Renault 5

By
Rebecca Faller

RENAULT 5

ISBN – 978-1-919663-47-0

Acknowledgements
Cover Art : Sarah Devincenzi & Sarah Radford
Graphics: Wallace McDougall
Editorial: Lydia Barrett & Conchita Triay
Photo: Vera Francis for Pozitive Rayz

Also by the author
The Civil Garrison © Rebecca Faller 2004

Bound and printed by
Tipografia la Nueva s.l.
Calle Arapiles 11-A
11380 Tarifa - Spain

Dedicated
to
The Two Sarahs

Three English girls go on a weird road trip across Europe, sleeping in a red Renault 5

Set in a bygone era of the early '90s with no mobile phones, email or sat nav, three young, single women decide to leave England and embark on a continental road trip. They save up some cash, buy an old Renault 5 and get on the ferry to France two days before Christmas, much to the amusement and disdain of family and friends. Over the course of the next six months the car becomes their home while they travel to France, Andorra, Spain, Gibraltar, Morocco and Portugal meeting colourful characters and experiencing good old-fashioned sex, drugs & rock 'n' roll… and even true love. Every night the girls chronicle their adventures in diaries along with sketches and cartoons of the places and the people they meet. This autobiographical novella combines those three diaries in an authentic, comical and detailed account of life in a small car.

Chapter One
The Coal Exchange

English villages, towns and cities are known for their pubs. Our small town, Emsworth in Hampshire was infamous for the fact that when I was living there and growing up in the '70s and '80s there were fifteen pubs in total ranging from family establishments with 'Beer Gardens' to haunts only frequented by Squaddies, or 'man bars' where women, children (and indeed Squaddies) were not welcome. The Coal Exchange in South Street, with its green-tile-fronted splendour, was a 'man bar' which sold real ales; in the '80s my friends and I wouldn't have been seen dead in there as it was full of fishermen and old Emsworth types, with surnames like Kennett and Marshall, but this was 1990, a new decade. Sark, Flee and I were of the opinion that it was now cool to forego all the popular havens full of annoying people we wanted to avoid and decided to start braving it and make The Coal Exchange our pub of choice. It was still full of fishermen and old Emsworth types, with surnames like Kennett and Marshall, but the 'Coal Hole' as it was now dubbed, was a place where the hip set went; young people who drank pints of HSB and smoked rollies; the 'new-hippies' of our generation who attended the University of Life and most definitely did not work at IBM or The National Westminster Bank.

Sark (Sarah Clarke) was the first person I ever met at Emsworth Infant School and she was seconded to look after me, and look after me she did as we sat next to one another all the way through Infant, Middle and Comprehensive school. Sarah was much taller than I was and had size 3 feet at the age of 5. She had read all the books in the reading cupboard and was the eldest girl in the class; clever, witty, loud she was, just the sort of person you wanted as a best friend. It was when we moved to Emsworth Middle School that a new girl from Essex came to town; she was pretty, artistic and wore fashionable clothes that her Mum made for her. Sarah Gee (Flee) was taken under our wing and the three of us began our relationship which would take us to such foreign destinations as Spain, Portugal, Gibraltar, Morocco, France and even Wales. We spent birthdays at grotty pubs in Havant or nightclubs in Pompey; New Year's Eves in London and Brighton; Easters in Cardigan Bay and all of it narrated by constant chatter and analysis of our lives, laughs and loves and how Maggie Thatcher was a man in drag and that we'd never go out with a Tory, ever. In 1990 we were proper wimmin and we'd educated ourselves despite having to attend the uninspiring Warblington 'Warbo' School and the lacklustre Southdowns College to do our A Levels. None of us had gone to university. We sort of wanted to, our parents wanted us to, but the Government had introduced tuition fees and unless you did a degree that was going to give you a proper job, like working in The National Westminster Bank or becoming a doctor or teacher, then forget it. Our parents were not going to fund our under-graduate education and all the spurious expenses that that may have involved. We were all three of us artistes, darling! Sark and Flee painted and sculpted and drew things in sketch pads and I trod the boards and sang at musical soirees. There was no way any of us were going to be able to get a proper job to pay back those fees so we all shelved that idea and did our own thing, we wanted to be different. Sark was living in Southsea and working as a sign writer, Flee had just moved back from London after splitting up with her childhood love, Paul Churchill; she was reluctantly back at her parents' house and working at Sainsbury's on the checkout and I was living in Brighton, on the dole.

Three single women in the summer of 1990, sitting in The Coal Exchange on a Saturday night, looking de rigueur and trying to avoid the inevitability of some tedious blokes, friends of Flee's brother, coming over and talking to us. We supped up sharpish, staggered back to Flee's parents' house and put the kettle on. Out came the digestive biscuits from the same cupboard, in the same tin, in the same kitchen around the same table that we'd sat at as children of the '70s, wearing Holly Hobby-style dresses. Sark and Flee looked at me and looked at each other. There was a pause...they dunked their biscuits. A disgusting habit I didn't share!

"Beck, we've got something to tell you," they said almost in unison. "We've made a decision; we want to go to Israel and live in (on?) a kibbutz".

"WHAT?!" I then went into overdrive: "What do you want to do that for? Everybody does that, everyone goes and 'lives in a Kibbutz'. It's totally mad and you'll get bossed about by twatty Uni-heads and 'types' and you won't learn anything about the culture and it'll be like being in a self-imposed prison, and anyhow, you can't go away, what will I do without you?"

"Come with us."

"When are you going?"

"Dunno, when we've saved up enough money for the tickets."
"What brought this on?"
"We don't want to stay in England any more, we want to get away from here, escape, but we need to be able to work."
"I do too but not to a kibbutz in Israel, it's such a cliché, why don't we all go somewhere but not to a kibbutz."
"Okay, where then?"
"Not inter-railing."
"No!"
"Not back-packing and carrying all that stuff around like everyone else does."
"No!"
"France?"
"Where in France, what about work and money and all that?"
"There's this ex-lecturer of mine" I said, and ignored Flee's groan, "he has a cottage near Rouen. He says I could use it this Christmas, we've always said we want to get away for Christmas, away from the usual family stuff."
Wise old Flee piped up with "I think he wants you to go to that cottage Beck, not us". Of course I had never considered that angle; the guy was married and my lecturer for God's sake! I thought he was just being friendly and helpful but Flee was probably right, she always notices these things where I, in all my naivety, never do.
The next hour was spent thrashing out our germ of an idea:
Right, we'd go to France after Christmas and stay at this cottage for free - no, we would go BEFORE Christmas. We didn't want to spend another same-old Christmas separated due to the obligations of parents and house visits. After all, both Flee and Sark's parents lived in Emsworth where mine had decided to up-sticks and bugger-off to West Wales in 1988 and there was a 5 hour long-winded, M4-service-station-riddled drive separating us. No, we were leaving before Christmas 1990. We would buy a second hand car, we would get it insured for Europe and become members of the AA or the RAC. We would pack Flee's old 2-man tent in the boot with sleeping bags, rucksacks (in the boot not on our precious backs!) and we would get holiday insurance, do things properly, be sensible, order travellers' cheques, join the Youth Hostelling Association. That 2-man tent was only for emergencies. Maps needed to be bought and injections. Did we need injections for Europe? How much was this all going to cost? A pad and pen were found, a list was made; we did calculations.
"Marilyn and Nathan are going to stay at her parents' house near Paris for Christmas" I said.
"Maybe we can stay with them for a night or two" said Sark.
"Yeah, we can stay at your lecturer's house in Rouen, then go on to Paris, do a bit

of France, then Germany" Flee suggested.
"Don't want to go to Germany do we, it'll be full of ugly blonde blokes and fat women carrying beer steins," I moaned. "Can't we just skip Germany and go straight to Italy?"
"I wouldn't mind visiting Germany, what's wrong with blonde blokes?" Flee said.
"Thought we could go down to Spain after France, get a bit of sun."
And the conversation went on in this vein until we got down to brass tacks and mentioned money.
"Beck, you have to get a job!" sang the Greek chorus in Pam's kitchen.
"Get off the dole and get a job!" It was starting to sound like an '80s soundtrack.
"You have to get it now, Beck!"
"All right, all right. I'll go back to Brighton and I'll get a job on Monday".
We had a mere four months to save up about five-hundred quid each, spending money, get all that insurance cover, ferry tickets and we had to buy a car.
"My Mum is selling her Renault 5," said I.
"That old red thing?" they chimed.
My Mum had started driving lessons the year before. It was never going to happen but nevertheless I tried to 'be nice' and took her out for a lesson. She crashed my Dad's Vauxhall Viva (vinyl roof) up a grassy bank just outside Cilgerran and I broke my arm in the process of trying to grab the steering wheel. Not long after that she was knocked off her scooter (not her fault this time) and narrowly escaped death but was left with some disabilities that meant she could never drive again. My Dad had bought her an old second hand Renault 5 which now sat dormant in the lay-by outside their house. It was just a simple '5' - not a GT or a Sport but a basic 2-door hatchback. No cassette player, just a very basic radio and the front seats did not fold back onto themselves or recline, you would just hoik them up on their hinges and then squeeze into the back. We bought the Renault 5 for £200 and an exciting relationship began.

Chapter Two
Avez-vous une chambre?

I did go back to Brighton and I did get a job but I also stayed on the dole and was very naughty but in hindsight I never scabbed off the UK Government ever again so all's-square in my eyes. I worked at quite a posh Italian Restaurant, 'Mamma Mia', as their kitchen porter and, to this day, peeling potatoes in large quantities never fazes me. I met two interesting people: Yumi, the Japanese waitress, and Bruno the French waiter who had his own business, selling fake flowers, but liked to work on Friday nights just to meet new people. Bruno was gorgeous, beautiful, artistic and dashing and we became friends and I was smitten. Those were the days when partner meant 'business partner' as in JR Ewing off Dallas and his Stetson-wearing multi-million-dollar dealings, so when Bruno introduced me to a lovely older man with a moustache, I immediately thought board table and not bedroom. The penny dropped some weeks later and I simply decided that now was not the time to find the perfect bloke as I was just about to leave England anyway, so I enjoyed the friendship with Bruno and promised to send postcards from his native France.

Yumi and I spent those four working months learning about each other's culture; we did everything together; we ate midnight snacks of noodles with chopsticks and afternoon cream teas. I took her to London to meet my brother, Nathan, and his French girlfriend, Marilyn, and we snowballed on Hampstead Heath. She had moved to Brighton from Tokyo and was enrolled at the language school and worked at 'Mamma Mia' in the evenings. She was calm, placid, knew how to do a proper massage and clean your ears out with a long stick. Her landlord had the hots for her but she was way out of his league. She didn't want me to leave and the restaurant was closing for two weeks over Christmas so I asked her if she wanted to come along with us to France for a holiday adventure. Flee and Sark chorused with their "Yeah, it'll be good for a laugh!" - a statement which I would too often go along with, no matter what the life-changing consequences

would be...
We sorted out the insurance, the tickets, the maps, travellers' cheques, French Francs, those injections and I caught the train up to Carmarthen, where my Dad collected me in his Ford Cortina Mk4 (Cream). The drive back to their house involved him asking me why I had to leave before Christmas.
"Why the 23rd of December, can't you just go on Boxing Day?
"No, the whole point is to leave before Christmas and spend it somewhere else for a change."
"The war is starting in January, you'll all be sent back."
"What?"
"That's what they do in wars, they send all the tourists back home."
"It's not a real war, not a world war."
"Not yet, but it could be."
"Well, we'll chance it".
Flee and Sark were receiving the same grilling from their parents who were all duly ignored and brushed off with a flick of the wrist.
"We want to do something different for a change! God!!!"
I waved them goodbye from outside their house in Abercych and pegged it down to Pompey where I collected Sark & Flee and we had a night out in Havant and a last hurrah! Havant Wine Bar (or La Cage to give it its proper name), The Dolphin and then all back to someone's house in Leigh Park where I rekindled an ever-recurring passion with my childhood sweetheart Clive. "Unfinished business" the sage-like Flee would remark. I had finally won the kissing competition that we had set ourselves back in August. Even Yumi got in on that one. Final score: Sark 0, Yumi 2, Flee 4 and me 6, although Flee tried to garner triple points by demanding that shagging counted as 3 kisses which of course it didn't!
We packed up our car only allowing ourselves: 1 sleeping bag; 1 large rucksack; 1 small bag; 1 coat; 1 pair of jeans; 3 leggings; 4 long-sleeved t-shirts; 3 short-sleeved t-shirts; some vests and underwear and socks; 2 jumpers; 1 pair of boots; 1 pair of shoes, hat and gloves and toiletries. We had a small camping gas burner and some camping pots, a communal food bag and a library of books which we spread across the back shelf of the car. We all bought a diary and pens to record our adventures and sketch pads and paints. The final and most important part of our luggage was the battery powered cassette player and a selection of tapes. We were strict. We all took exactly £500 each. Sark and I were still scarred from the time we went on a holiday to Milan back in 1987 with a third person, who not only took double the money we had but subsequently gloated, bought herself luxuries and never shared them with us. We hated her! Flee's ex-boyfriend Paul had laughed at us; everyone had laughed at us in fact. "Five hundred quid? You'll be back by January". Paul and his very handsome but aloof older brother,

Matthew, had 'gone travelling' earlier in the summer and didn't get past the beaches of France and les jeunes filles where they had blown all their money on champagne; they were back within a fortnight. We rather liked the idea that everyone was simultaneously shaking their heads either in front of us or when we weren't there: they are mad, they haven't thought this through, they haven't even got anywhere to stay in France. Yep, Flee was right, that old lecturer of mine and his quaint cottage in Rouen never happened, his thatched roof had apparently "blown off in a storm" and he was waiting for the repairs so "no cottage, sorry". We did scurry around to some travel agents prior to leaving to try and get accommodation in Dieppe but zilch. "You're just like Jesus, Mary and Joseph, no room in the inn at Christmas," remarked the girl behind the desk at Thomas Cook. So glad I was leaving England...

The night before beginning our adventure, we all slept at my old lodgings in Elm Grove, Brighton, where Ruth and Simon were kind enough to let us all kip for our final night. We packed up the car and it was raining. We hadn't correctly gauged the lack of interior space so shoved all our rucksacks on the roof rack and then had to try and waterproof them by covering them with a few ripped-apart black bin liners squeezed underneath some stretched-to-the-limit octopus straps. You could hear the black plastic flapping away in the wind as we sped down the A259 to Newhaven.

You never really know you suffer from sea-sickness until you are in the middle of the sea on a boat with nowhere to run to for respite, apart from the vomit-coated toilets that is. I turned green apparently, I was amusing apparently. I had this notion of us sitting in the ferry bar drinking French beer and munching away on baguettes in celebration of our great escape but the reality was me sitting up on deck, freezing, shivering and willing the French coastline to hasten its way towards us and get me off these choppy seas.

Adjusting to driving on the wrong side of the road isn't fun in the rain with steamed up wing mirrors in a top-heavy Renault 5 in France, with English plates. People pointed at us and laughed! Dieppe was very much like Chichester and not the 'filthy port' everyone said it was going to be. We parked up and walked around the town and all the hotels we first encountered were closed. It was starting to get dark and we decided it was about time we tried to speak some French. Our French was atrocious. I knew I was rubbish ever since I mis-translated that Jimmy Somerville song Comment te dire adieu and thought that 'Derrière un Kleenex' meant something about wiping your bum with paper until Sark said it must mean 'from behind a tissue' in reference to crying. Sark had Grade II CSE and was okay, Flee had an O Level but was too shy and Yumi was a non-starter. I hated languages at school and didn't even take an exam but was ready to learn with the aid of their knowledge and our phrase book. We tried a couple of places but they were either full or too expensive. Some kind soul back in England had given us a guidebook on cheap travel called 'Let's Go France '88!' so we looked up Dieppe in the index and were directed to Hôtel La Jetée, 5 rue de l'aisle Thomas. Sark and I went in and were warmly welcomed by a middle-aged woman with a white cat. Sark was understood perfectly and managed to negotiate a room for four, at 185 Francs for the night. We got Flee and Yumi from the car and then struggled with our bags up teeny-tiny stairs to a room right up in the attic. It was everything we had naively imagined; a French attic room with lovely iron bedsteads, a bathtub along the hall and a dormer window which overlooked the rooftops and the port of Dieppe, an idyll from one of those French films we three liked to watch on Channel 4, and all for peanuts. We sneakily smuggled in our little camping gas burner and a saucepan and Flee cooked us up tinned tomato soup with cheese and biscuits followed by Jaffa Cakes. Bruno had gifted me a bottle of Asti-Spumanti so we cracked that open and laughed about the day. We'd finally left England and were in France and tomorrow was Christmas Eve.

We woke up at 10.30am and had to share each other's water, in the bath down the hall as there was not enough hot water for all four of us. Yumi was merrily going along with all our foibles and had fitted in well so far. We ate a fruit-dash breakfast and went down into the lobby and spoke to the husband of the woman with the white cat and found out her name was Isobel (the woman not the cat). We christened the husband 'Monsieur Hotel' and had a Harpo Marx-style conversation with him replete with whistles and mime. We decided to stay two more nights if possible and then move on in the direction of Paris. My brother, Nathan, was spending Christmas there at Marilyn's Mum's house, just outside the city and we planned to meet up with them. Monsieur Hotel offered us 'Room 4' which was up fewer flights of stairs and was remarkably cheaper. We ventured out on a trip to Mammoth hypermarket, the sort of place that people from college visited on booze-cruises. We all smoked and the fags were only £1 a packet over there and, if you smoked those revolting French brands, they were even cheaper. We stocked up on fags and food and went back to the hotel to make ourselves cheese and jam baguettes. In the afternoon we sauntered round Dieppe, which was all abuzz for Christmas Eve: lots of fresh fish stalls; oysters and mussels and special cakes in the patisserie windows. We wanted to do a recce and find a decent looking bar in which to spend our Christmas Eve. We got an idea of where the action may take place later and then went up to the Chateau which was closed but impressive nonetheless. I made Christmas Eve dinner which was baked beans and a carrot each. Yumi had bought us a Marks & Sparks Christmas cake and some wine that her landlord had given her, so we drank it and started to sing carols. Yumi sang us a Japanese song. We erected our own homemade tree which we made with wrapping paper and stuck it to the wall with half-sticky tape and put all our presents beneath it. We were in full swing with the singing when we were interrupted by a knock at the door. It must be Monsieur Hotel coming to tell us off so we hurriedly bundled away the cooking evidence and opened up. It was Monsieur Hotel but he was smiling and carrying a bottle of wine with four glasses. He opened the wine and poured it for us and we wished him a joyeux Noël and thanked him. He left and we broke into more singing this time with percussion and then there was another knock at the door. It was a girl with a Christmas table cloth for us to use tomorrow she said. More Harpo Marxing and she left. We plaited Flee's hair and Yumi twisted my hair up into Mickey Mouse ears, très chic. Sark and I suggested that we go to the local Church Saint Jacques for the Christmas Eve service. Flee hated all things church: "subservient Catholics queuing up humbly for confession", but I saw it as 'cultural' so we frog-marched Flee and Yumi down there. The lengthy service went from bad to worse, not the sort of thing we were used to at Emsworth Baptist Church at all but we did get the chance to sing along to a few French hymns which were handily printed on a sheet of paper. We noticed that it seemed okay to leave the Church before the service had finished, because other local people were doing so, and we followed suit and scarpered guiltily with heads bowed. It turned out that the Church was the swingingest place in town because the rest of Dieppe was DEAD. We were not used to this on Christmas Eve. Havant this was not, no crowds squeezed into The Six Bells, no fights in the chinky after closing, nothing was open! We wandered around the streets and finally came upon a red glow down a back street; it was called 'Scottish Pub' of all things. Upon entering we were met with a sea of tartan, flags, upholstered banquettes, bar stools, tartan carpet but not a Scotsman in sight. We were the only people in there. We ordered four beers at the bar and in doing so witnessed funny looks from the barmaid. Three French blokes came in and the essence of an atmosphere was brewing finally. Ten minutes later the barmaid appeared at our table with four more beers and nodded in the direction of the three smiling Frenchmen. We grinned out a Merci to them with finger-waves all round but that was it because of the language barrier. They bought us two more rounds in the course of the evening and by midnight the place was full and we were all pissed and singing Beatles songs and there was even a bit of an attempt at some dancing at one point, although not by us. All in all a good bit of Christmas Eve merriment and we realised that in France you don't order at the bar, you wait to be served at table.

Christmas Day 1990. I got up first and made the others some tea. We had breakfast; fruit and yogurt and then opened our presents. I was blackballed on this one as my tradition is: 'No presents until all the washing up has been done after eating the Christmas Dinner!' But I was willing to forget my own family's traditions and try something new. My Mum had knitted us all bed socks with matching woolly hats; Flee's Mum had given us some more cake, Sark's parents, biscuits. Ostentatious hats were created out of the left-over wrapping paper and we all put them on to get into the spirit of things and proceeded to decorate our Christmas table with the donated cloth from last night and a few candles. Suddenly Sark let out a scream and pointed to my head yelling "your hat has caught fire!" I whipped it off my head and we all stamped on top of it and I was in a state of shock because my hair nearly went up in flames. It was amusing though and I was known for the rest of Christmas Day 1990 as 'The Human Candle'. Further jocularity ensued days later when we were playing a tape of L.A Woman by The Doors in the car and there's that line in the title track 'I see your head is burning'. Oh how we laughed! That Christmas Day was spent in a manner befitting Victorian England. We had an old book of Charles Dickens Christmas Stories and I read aloud 'The Seven Poor Travellers' after which we had our grand Christmas lunch of sesame sticks, bread sticks, herb biscuits and sliced carrots, with peanut butter. We opened wine and started on a main of tinned ratatouille with Edam cheese arranged on top, in a star shape, and proper bread. Our afternoon was spent quietly playing cards and discussing where the hell we were going to stay the following night. Supper at 9pm was more bread sticks, peanut butter and jam with cake. Sark told me that Jamaica ginger cake was lovely if spread with peanut butter. It wasn't, but I ate it anyway. We had considered going for a 'bracing Christmas stroll' but it was raining and windy and cold. We rounded off the evening with a Dickens ghost story and Flee said it was the most enjoyable Christmas she'd had in years because she felt like a child all over again.

Chapter Three
I Love Paris in the Springtime

Boxing Day is not a holiday in France which meant that the shops were open and we could stock up on grub and fags. We had a last bath in our commune-style chain, tidied up and paid Isobel for the room. We drove off in the direction of Rouen ,which we had heard was 'bloody expensive for accommodation'. Shame about that lecturer and his picturesque cottage with the thatched roof. Bet he was shacked up in there with some eager and willing student, thatched roof intact. We thought we'd have 'a bit of old Edith' to start off our French adventure and stuck in a tape. The first song was 'L'Homme a La Moto' and it set the scene with its racing 'hit the road at great speed' melody. Rouen is famously known as the place where Joan of Arc got burnt at the stake and now on that place of her death, a modernist ('daring' the guidebook said) church Sainte-Jeanne d'Arc has been built with a fabulous spiky roof under which we sheltered from the torrential rain. The jutting-out points of the structure are meant to evoke the flames of the death hearth that consumed poor old Joan. It really was impressive, Sark hated it, Flee loved it and I thought it was evil. The rain stopped and we decided to cave-in to a patisserie visit. It had to be done. The woman behind the counter was a grumpy old bag but we bought a flute and some cakes and returned to Joan's church and ate them under the flames. By coincidence we saw an English bloke who had helped us buy a travel plug in Mammoth's, on Christmas Eve, but we ignored him. We camped outside the Tourist Information Office waiting for it to open and got approached by a strange youth asking for cigarettes who kept trying to kiss us and told us he was in the army. He fell in love with Sark and handed her two scrawled addresses for her to write to him at. She had to push him off her in the end, with a booming "Au revoir!" He tried to follow us down the road but we escaped him. We bought two more gas bottles for 20 francs and left Rouen, deciding it was far too twee for us; the Lewes of France in our opinion and it had bad vibes. We needed to get on the road and find a campsite so we took the main roads and looked out for any signs, driving for miles through wintry countryside with all those avenues of trees that kept Napoleon's armies under shade as they marched. The trees had no leaves but we used our imaginations. I was allowed to choose the music as I had the cassette player on my lap. I had to be careful not to play any scary stuff when it was dusk or nightfall as Sark gets the willies so no Tom Waits and definitely not 'Mr Kite' from Sgt Peppers because that gives her "nightmares about tea cups with legs that can walk". The sun had not set so I chanced it with Raindogs. We saw a sign with tents so campsites were coming up. The first one we arrived at was full of gypsy-looking dwelling places and totally filthy with no facilities at all, and the second was out in the middle of a field. I knocked on the door and got shouted at by a moody hag woman: "Camping fermé!" We managed to use their toilets though and then drove on to a village called Boos and stopped at a shop. No bread, no peanut butter, no marmite and nowhere to sleep for the night! We kept driving towards the next village in the vain hope of seeing a campsite sign and got to Fluery-sur-Andelle where we turned off the main road to the desolate village of Radepont which was about half a mile long. We parked the car near a farm and made a unanimous decision that we would just stop here for the night and sleep in the car. We ate our dinner of bread and cheese and had a game of cards and then drove back to Fluery-sur-Andelle to warm ourselves up in a bar. The first one was like a pub and we ordered four coffees. I phoned Nathan from a booth inside the bar which meant that I could hear him. The village idiot latched onto us and we bought two more coffees each while his equally repulsive bearded mate came over and kissed us all. We couldn't understand each other so the whole effort was pointless. We managed to get away from them and went to an hotel for another coffee and sat chatting and making our drinks last. Who should walk in but the village idiot again? He tried to buy us a drink but we left immediately and went to a restaurant bar for a final coffee before going to the car. We started the ignition and who should appear but the bearded kissing monster! We drove off before he saw us and returned to our spot by the woods and the farm and parked the car for the night.

Don't ever sleep in your car in the middle of nowhere by a dark forest, even if you do have three mates with you. It was the worst night of my life, lying there awake thinking that all the others were asleep and spaced-out on too many coffees and not enough food. The trees started to come alive in the fog. It was warm in the car but totally uncomfortable trying to get to sleep in a sitting position. At about midnight a police car crawled past slowly, shone its lights on us and then passed. Phew! It turned out that we were all awake thinking the same thing and shivering from fear in our sleeping bags. In the bright winter sun of the morning everything looked glorious again and we put the experience behind us. The car was all damp and condensed and we ached like hell. We bought some bread from the mobile shop and had breakfast in the car and then drove towards Paris full speed ahead. We got to the outskirts at midday and decided to head towards Versailles and visit the palace. We couldn't afford to go inside the actual palace building so spent ages wandering around the gardens. It was the most amazing place I had ever seen, pink marble, girt fountains and canals; you could just stand there at the top of the steps and see for miles; beautifully structured lakes and gardens in perfect symmetry, my type of thing. It was sunny and clear so we explored the forests to find the summer house of Marie-Antoinette. At that time the rain was coming down in large hailstones but we were sheltered by all the trees and when we saw the little set of fairytale, gingerbread cottages, we didn't give a shit about the weather because the atmosphere was so magical. It was not real there in the forest, the architecture and mood giving us a feeling of being taken back years in a time machine. We walked around the rest of the place in a complete daze, shocked in fact. The last thing we saw was the Bassin de Neptune, sculptures of Neptune all muscular and bearded with giant fish and horses bursting out of a lake. Hectic, but I loved it.

We returned to the car via Tourist Information who told us about a campsite nearby so we drove there just as dusk was setting in. It was 100F for one night plus a tent for four people, a bit 'prixy' but who cares. We started to put up our tent and discovered that a crucial pole was missing: shit, merde, porco dio, whatever you like to call it. I used my charm on the campsite bloke who let us use one of his massive, static bungalow tents for no extra charge so we got unpacked and started to prepare dinner.

"We're fucking freezing our girts off!" we three moaned. Yumi was starting to learn our southern slang and was mastering the accent.

"Girts?" she inquired.

"Hello!" a jolly voice boomed in our tent entrance. "What are you doing, my name is Thierry".

A tall skinny bloke in his late twenties with thick, curly brown hair stood before us watching us cook dinner.

"Dinner?" he said. "Very nice, are you English?"

"Yes"

"Are you on holiday?"

"Sort of".

"Too cold for holiday, hahahaha!"

Thierry (we called him Terry because it suited his personality more) was a 'traveller cum forest worker' and told us that he lived full time in a ridge tent on the campsite but had decided to squat in one of the other static bungalow tents next to ours. He seemed quite cheery but a bit of a nutter. It was refreshing to talk to someone in English, anyone in fact. Tonight was so cold, the coldest night I had ever experienced, worse than the New Years Eve Sark and I spent in Flee & Paul's old front room, in Leyton, with no heating and using unlined nylon curtains as a duvet. Our tent had a broken zip and the draught was coming in. I went to bed wearing two pairs of socks, leggings, jeans, two t-shirts, a polo-neck jumper AND a balaclava and I was still cold inside my sleeping bag. This feeling made sleeping inside the car seem like a hotel. We all tried to sleep but couldn't. We could hear Terry talking to someone really loudly, shouting even. He kept doing this at intervals but then we thought that maybe he was talking to himself! We kept laughing about him for ages and then heard a very loud, angry voice boom out "SHUT UP!! I've got to work in the morning – fucking shit!" We immediately silenced ourselves and shivered in our beds. This guy was a bit mad; we'd figured that one out by now. After about five minutes of silence we heard a zip opening and noise just outside our area. Again I thought everyone else was asleep and just shit myself hiding inside my sleeping bag. I heard noises around the side of our tent and banging sounds with footsteps. I tried to block them out of my mind but sleeping is so difficult in situations like this.

The next morning we discovered that we'd all heard the noises during the night but were too scared to speak. We were so rubbish! We thought that maybe he'd nicked our stuff or something but it was all still there. We put it behind us and got on with the day but then had an accident with our gas bottle and wasted a whole canister of gas whilst trying to change it over. It started fizzing and spinning around and we all ran away from it screaming. Sark booted it into the bushes which was brave of her and we became rather hysterical and had to move to another bungalow for fear of blowing ourselves up. It was Sark's turn to drive today. She and I were the only ones who could drive so we took it in turns; one day on, one day off. The car wouldn't start but Terry came to the rescue. We didn't say a word about last night and it was all smiles and waves. We all went to the campsite showers (hot showers oh bliss!) and as I was all soaped up Terry burst in on me pretending he had 'got the wrong door' and no mention of the wrong actual changing room altogether. He was promptly shooed out of the place by the others who found it hilarious. Later on we found out that Terry had a skeleton key and then I got bitten on the leg by a campsite dog and was glad to see the back of that place.

We drove towards St. Germain de la Grange where Marilyn's parents lived and stopped off in the dead-end town of Plaisir (no it was not thank you!) and had a coffee in a bustling cafe full of moustachioed French stereotypes and cheeky barmen. We used the phone to call Marilyn (not in), then my Dad (he's all right) and then my pen friend Lionel. Lionel was a black ballet dancer whom I'd met on a theatrical workshop in Moscow in 1990. He was part of a troupe of French dancers and we arranged to meet at the foot of Tour Montparnasse the next day at 6 o'clock. Paris was now drawing excitingly close and I couldn't wait to get there. Sark visited when she was a child aged 10 and I remember her snootily proclaiming at school, "I went to France for my holiday, the beaches were nice but Paris was a slum, urgh!"

I finally got in touch with Marilyn and she said that because we were so near why didn't we all go round there and stay the night because her parents were away. Hooray, hot food and a proper bed. We couldn't find the house and drove around for ages so I stopped at a phone box to call and met a girl who spoke English and had lived in Brighton. She took me to her house where I ended up conversing with her parents who phoned Marilyn and pointed us in the right direction, basically just across the street. What luxury! Open fires, leather sofas, two dogs, a cat, aperitifs, wine, a leg of lamb studded with garlic. We all got sozzled and fell into our beds.

The next day we all awoke with fuzzy heads but in comfort, apart from Flee who was awoken to the sounds of Marilyn and Nathan having sex. Marilyn really helped us out and made a million telephone calls to try and find us somewhere to stay. After many, many rejections we managed to locate a place in the deep southern suburbs of Paris, a youth hostel at 30F per night in the town of Arpajon so we bade our farewells to Nathan & Marilyn and headed south. Today was a horrible, horrible day. Not long after leaving, Nathan and Marilyn, we passed a fatal car accident on the road. We saw one of the victims slouched over his steering wheel and the other car was in a complete mess, rolled over in the ditch. The ambulances were late coming and all the people were in the road directing the traffic and trying to sort out the victims. It was bloody awful and gave me the shakes. I couldn't concentrate on driving but I had to put it out of my mind. We were on the road at 2pm but didn't get to our destination until 6pm, a journey that should have taken one hour. When we got to the hostel I had a minor argument with the manageress about the price differences. We were also supposed to be in central Paris right NOW to meet Lionel and they were wasting our time! We got to Tour Montparnasse two hours late and obviously he wasn't there so we phoned him and arranged to meet on Monday at 1pm. We passed another fatal accident on the roads to Paris, crazy drivers everywhere. We had a coffee at the nearest bar, got back in the car and attempted to drive back but got lost again. Eventually we found the right road and thought it would be plain sailing until we passed yet another fatal smash-up and about 100 metres further there was a corpse in the middle of the road. I slammed on my brakes in the middle of the motorway, Sark screamed, "Put on your hazards!!!" I fumbled around and found the button just as the car behind us had to slam on their brakes before smashing into us. The corpse was that of a very large dog with its brains hanging out, a

Great Dane Sark observed. I couldn't run over it because of its size and I also thought it was human from a distance. We drove back the rest of the way slowly and shakily. We arrived at the Youth Hostel and made some hot food in their communal kitchen. We sat up till midnight writing our diaries.
This was the sort of Youth Hostel where you sleep on a grubby mattress in a room full of strangers and then get locked out of the place after breakfast; unable to return until teatime, but it was all we could afford in Paris (or even the suburbs of Paris). This morning we had concentrated tomato soup for breakfast and decided we needed to stock up on food. We had to wait for the bloody woman to get out of bed so we could book a room for that night as they didn't do advance bookings. We got the hell out of there and legged it to Paris. No accidents today and a straight run up to the Porte D'Ivry with Regatta de Blanc on our tape player. We parked the car at Euromarche and got on the metro for the first time which we found surprisingly easy to use. We headed for the Champs-Élysées and l'Arc de Triomphe, nicked some maps from Tourist Information and went to the toilet in McDonalds. We had read that all museums were free on a Sunday but sadly found that none of them were. We walked for miles being rejected at gallery doors because we were not paying 25F a throw; goodness me! After gawping at La Tour Eiffel we got on a bus so we could see more sights. We queued up for Le Louvre (or La Looboo as Yumi pronounced it), saw the Mona Lisa and Venus de Milo and the other famous paintings. Le Louvre is massive.
"I thought it was going to be a backstreet town house with the Mona Lisa over a fireplace and a couple of sculptures dotted around" I said to the others.
"What? You didn't realise it was this big" they retorted with disgust (artists).
After wandering along a maze of corridors, we couldn't really be bothered to see the whole lot. I did like Delacroix though, and those really, really massive paintings especially that one off the Pogues album cover Rum, Sodomy and the Lash. Later on we bought a baguette at Pyramides metro station for 15F then headed for the Pompidou Centre, walking through busy streets and lanes where Flee and I shared a chocolate crepe which was delicious and hot. The Pompidou Centre was not really my cup of tea; a modern big thing with escalators in plastic tunnels going up the outside of the building to the top where we experienced excellent views of Paris. I suffered from acute vertigo and couldn't go anywhere near the edge without turning green. Sark and Flee amused themselves by pushing me towards the edge and running away! There was street theatre outside and colourful fountains and a great atmosphere. After recovering from my retreat from those literally dizzy heights we took it easy with a slow amble over the bridges of the Seine to Notre Dame and went inside. You entered the cathedral through massive old doors with a rush of incense to the nostrils. The place was quite eerie with lots of arches and gargoyles, exactly what one would expect but

impressive all the same. It was dark by now and the Christmas lights were all switched on, the ones in the trees and on the façade of Galeries Lafayette were particularly stunning. We got the bus to Porte Royale, and then the metro. Sark had to jump over the barrier because her ticket got stuck and Flee got asked to be a model by a bloke on the train who gave her his photographer's calling card. Mmmmm. Paris, what a wonderful city and we'd so much more to see. Sark remarked that all the women wore "dodgy fur coats and brown lipstick" and she had a point. Exhausted we drove back to Arpajon. The dead dog had been moved to the side of the road now. That evening we ate tinned ratatouille and beans for dinner, accompanied by the head-splitting sound of a twat playing the bongos.

New Year's Eve 1990. At the hostel was a dodgy bossy man (whom we nicknamed 'Bossy') who was just a simple tenant like us but thought that because he was thirtysomething he could order the rest of us around and get first dibs with the cooking utensils. Sark had the pleasure of viewing his buttocks in the morning. Later on we had a rendezvous with Lionel and a New Year's Dinner hosted by Laurent, Marilyn's brother who lives in Nation. We cobbled together clothing for a New Year's Eve party which was not easy as our wardrobes were limited and we slapped on a bit of make-up to make us look at least alive. Didn't want Lionel seeing us looking so rough. We drove into the city and finally timed our meeting with Lionel correctly. Lionel looked good as always - very à la mode Flee said, with his cheeky grin and infectious laugh. The others didn't find him annoying and theatrical which I was a bit concerned about.

"Are you sure he's not gay, Beck?" Flee asked

"He's got a girlfriend."

"Doesn't mean a thing."

Lionel gave us a walking tour of trendy artistic Paris and then took us to the cafe of the moment, Cafe Costes in Les Halles. 1920s style decor; ultra modern; people staring at our total un-chicness. We were actually quite chic back in England with the aid of our wardrobes and decent hair products but now we all looked like Sue from Eastenders, wearing regulation black or washed-out purples, with miserable screwed-up faces because of the cold. The girls in there heard us speak and then unanimously French-shrugged in relief, "Oh zey are Eeenglish". Lionel insisted that we go in just to see the toilets if nothing else. They were amazing: weird and mirrored and Sark got lost in them - who really wants to see themselves pissing anyway, especially from six angles? The bill was 110F for four coffees. "Lordy Dordy!" but Lionel paid for the lot; he was really looking after us. After that brief episode of frivolity, we kissed Lionel goodbye on both cheeks and drove towards Nation and parked by the metro station Alexandre Dumas. We were quite a bit early for dinner so we sat in the car and admired the beautiful iron

art-deco entrance whilst at the same time being party to some unexpected entertainment. The florist opposite was run by a gigantic queen of a man, flabby, flamboyant and with a Kevin Keegan curly mullet and bushy tash. He wore a black jogging suit, had a butch Alsatian dog and a Latin-look toy boy and we watched as he camped it up, around pots of irises and buckets of roses. We wound our windows down so we could hear what he was saying and the tone of his voice; all gasps and jazz-hands. We christened him Fatty the Florist. He suddenly noticed us all staring at him so he then began gossiping and stage-whispering into the toy boy's ear and then to the wine man next door. We were laughing at him skipping off to answer the telephone but later when our car wouldn't start he was laughing at us and then flounced over to the bonnet giving it what he called his "magic touch" which miraculously worked. We were firm friends after that and waved him a fond goodbye as we drove down the road towards 12 rue de Charrones. Sark later sketched his image in her diary in honour of his amusement.
Laurent was a lovely bloke, with a lovely voice, with a lovely flat and we all fell in love with him. He and Marilyn presented us with a splendid 5-course meal which lasted for four hours. At one point Nathan asked us to smell one of the cheeses:
"Go on, sniff that, it smells like your bum when you put your finger in it," he said and passed it around under our noses giggling.
"Nathan! Don't touch the cheese!" Marilyn screamed.
To this day it is our trademark one-liner for any Marilyn impressions. At midnight they turned off all the lights and started screaming out of the windows which we all thought was a bit strange (we pronounced it strang-gee) but followed suit and then ran down into the streets to greet neighbours with "bonne année!" We all wanted to kiss Laurent more than once but were given our perfunctory rations and skulked back up to the flat. The next step was to drive (yes drive in our car), to a party at a flat somewhere near Sacre Coeur. We arrived at 3am. Nice old flat, free booze and nibbles, but terrible music which kept being changed mid-song with long gaps in between. Finally someone had the foresight to stick on 'I've Got The Power' by Snap! and the floor filled up with boppers. There was a lot of that hoppy French dancing going on and a fat show-off who kept screaming "Sex Machine!" which is exactly what he wasn't. He spoke English in an American accent and he was too much by the time it got to 6am.We all had a bit of a boogie and left; where were all the dishy French blokes we were told about? We drove aimlessly around the Périphérique and saw yet another crash involving five cars and the streets were still packed. We got lost on the way home so many times because I was seeing double and couldn't navigate that in the end we pulled into any old car park and I fell asleep. End of 1990, what would 1991 bring?

Chapter Four
I Love Paris in the Fall

1991 and I woke up slumped behind the wheel of a Renault 5, with a bad back. On special occasions such as New Year's Day, the Hostel Hag let us stay indoors all day. Mind you, this meant that the whole motley crew of tenants were also inside and we had to elbow our way onto a table in order to sit down and eat. We obviously had hangovers from hell as did they, and we solemnly played cards and ate pasta while that bongo bloke was there banging away with an inane look on his face. Okay, he did look like the split of Michael Hutchence and caught our eye at first but then we just hated him with venom and kept flicking him the evils but he just kept on playing like the violinists on the Titanic. Old Bossy was now sleeping in a tent outside so was no longer getting on our tits. "Be thankful for small mercies," as my Mother would always say. They were playing a U2 album over and over. "One of the shit ones" Flee said; "They're all shit," I said.

January 2nd and it was back to business with a trip to Orleans, birth place of poor old Joan, burned by the fiery flames of hell. We now realised that some sights were free to enter like cathedrals and the like, but also some museums, so first stop in a new town was always Tourist Information to find out what was free-gratis. Apart from the Russian photography exhibition, Musée Beaux Arts was nothing special - the usual pictures of fat, powdered men who look like other people we know: "He looks like your uncle, Beck."

The cathedral was awesome in comparison, better even than Notre Dame in Paris and Sark lit a candle in St. Christopher's Shrine "just in case" she said. I phoned Mum, Lionel and Laurent today and we decided not to go back to Arpajon but save money and just sleep in the car.

The hostel would be okay if they didn't lock you out but for the prices they charged we'd rather by-pass nights in the dorms, with groups of odd people, and sleep upright in our car. We decided that we would change tack and park-up in some suburban cul-de-sac rather that down a rural country lane; the street lamps gave us a sense of security and by the morning the car was all steamed up anyway so nobody knew there were four girls kipping inside and anyone who saw us earlier on must have thought it was strange, a Renault 5 full of giant caterpillars. It worked and we all slept very well but now we had to try and find a bar with a sink inside the toilet cubicle so we could each go and have a private 'pits & bits' strip wash. We drove into the Champagne region towards Reims, had coffee in the theatre bar at Sens then stomped around Napoleon's Chateau in Fontainbleu which was a bit too shabby for our liking. We stood and spoke to peacocks in the rain for ten minutes and a bar-owner took the piss out of us. We groaned outside the mouth-watering patisserie windows and kept seeing Gallettes du Roi which were large round cakes with crowns on them. A waitress explained that they were for a celebration in a few days' time for the Three Kings and that these traditional cakes had presents inside them. We were starting to get rather choosy about how much we should pay for a coffee in the suburbs and we had decided on a maximum of 6F. All the bars had their drinks tariff displayed outside so we would peruse them before entering and move on where necessary. We had a staring competition tonight with a group of young boys in the town of Melun, sweet and shy as they were but far too young to be flirting with us! Then they were pushed aside by older versions who were all puke and uninteresting and when we left, the whole lot of them followed us down the street either by foot or by car. They were harmless and we shook them off and went back 'home' which was now our lovely Renault 5. Another wonderful night's sleep parked up in the Milton Keynes of France. Safety in suburbia.

After some research we discovered that you could have showers at Gare Montparnasse but they were 18F a pop. Too expensive, we had to find other ways to wash. A lot of the toilets were of the 'sit up and beg' variety, like a shower tray with a hole in it and two foot-shaped indentations where you stand and balance. Because the sinks were outside in the communal area, we could not even clean our teeth without attracting suspicion. We developed a system of finding a good place to park up for the night and then look for a bar which had the right coffee tariff AND a sink inside the toilet which we would then use as our morning bar. We would breakfast in the car which was always yoghurt followed by a 10cm (yes, identically measured) piece of baguette spread with a triangle of 'laughing cow' cheese, la vache qui rit in France; La vaca que ríe in Spain; A vaca que ri in Portugal and Al-Baqara Ad-Dahika in Morocco. That cheese got everywhere and it formed part of our staple diet for the next few months. For lunch we would have the same sized piece of bread, no yoghurt though, but with added extras such as jam, peanut butter or marmite. For dinner we would have a slightly larger piece of bread and cheese but sometimes with a lettuce leaf shoved inside and on extravagant days even some sliced onions. It was too nippy to fire-up the gas burner in a Parisian car park so we stopped using it and just ate a bit of cold. We were all starting to lose weight; we smoked like chimneys and drank black coffee because it was much cheaper than Café crème. Flee was as skinny as a rake anyway, Sark and I were rather more voluptuous and she ended up losing 2-stone in four weeks on the laughing cow diet without doing any proper exercise, unless you count wandering around France and Spain as exercise. Sark could have sold her diet to a shit magazine or done a book deal and been on the telly promoting herself as The Laughing Cow incarnate.

Yumi was flying back to England on 8th January so we needed to stay in and around the Paris region much as we wanted to move down south to somewhere a bit warmer. I was waiting for a letter to arrive, something from the dole office that needed to be signed and sent back. Laurent had offered to have it sent to his home which suited us fine because it provided us with an excuse to drool over him again. At his place one evening, we sat for ages waiting for him to say "go and get your sleeping bags and kip on my floor" but he didn't. We devoured the nibbles he had laid out for us and drank his beer while he slowly sipped orange juice. When he started to yawn we decided it was never going to happen and left. Back in the car, we compared ourselves to lecherous builders, discussing our evening with Laurent and how he had spoken about the history of Paris in his adorable French accent.

"He's had a haircut," I remarked.

"He's got lovely hair" said Flee.

"His arms are incredibly sexy," we concurred.

"Nice eyes," Yumi noted.

"Nice hands," Sark added.

"Nice everything" someone said.

That night we slept outside an army barracks in Nation. The place was full of prostitutes and one in particular wearing stockings, suspenders, basque and a raincoat was the first to be picked up. I woke up the following morning in a warm pool of blood. In all the excitement I had forgotten about periods! This was going to be fun. It was high time we went to a launderette anyway. We drove to a place called Meaux and found one and spent an entire morning washing and tumbling and went to a bar and had a decent strip-wash. We hadn't had a hot meal for 4 days. I wasn't really missing food but I desperately wanted to wash my hair because it was now itching, not because of lice, simply because of dirt! There's an old wives' tale that claims if you never wash your hair it will eventually start washing itself naturally. It is simply not true, unless you leave it for months before the natural effect kicks in. I couldn't wait much longer.

I have always wanted to go and visit Edith Piaf's grave which is in Cimitière Le Père Lachaise on the east side of Paris. The place is so huge and higgledy-pi-

ggledy that they have produced a map of the site; we bought one for 10F and then earmarked all the graves we wanted to see plus others that we ticked off along the way. All the big guns of art, literature and music: Bizet, Maria Callas, Collete, Chopin, all that lot. We followed a graffiti trail to see our old friend and provider of "good shagging albums" (as Flee divulged); Jim Morrison. Seated on and around his grave were a couple of Dutch hippies and an American bloke with a guitar. What is it with the Dutch? Much like Australians they seem to crop up when you least expect them. They were all drinking cans of lager and shaking their heads in a solemn fashion bemoaning the death of their God ,whilst attempting to knock-out some Doors numbers but none of them could actually string together a full line of a song. They were the beatnik equivalent of pub singers: Come On Baby Light My Fire! With eyebrows raised, we left them to it and moved on to the beautifully minimalist tombstone of our old mucker and provider of pithy one-liners Oscar Wilde (a handbag?!). Edith's grave didn't disappoint. Covered with fresh flowers, as if she'd just popped her clogs last week and lots of people crowding around. The pièce de résistance had to be the tomb of Victor Noir, scene of 'erotic erosion'. Marilyn had told us that we must see this grave. Legend has it that Victor was a young Casanova who had an affair with his mate's wife and then died in the resulting duel aged 22. His life-size bronze statue lies atop his coffin, his trouser button undone with his top-hat upturned beside him; he has a notable erection. Myth says that placing a flower in the upturned top hat, after kissing the statue on the lips. will bring a husband within the year, fertility and wonderful orgasms. For years women have gone to the grave at night and 'made lurve' to Victor thus the reason for his lips, erection and boot-toes being noticeably shinier than the rest of the statue.
"Shall we kiss him?" I asked.
"Nah, I'm not kissing a statue you weirdo" gasped Sark
"Full or germs" said Flee.
Yumi just shook her head and laughed and I did the honours - it had to be done! Flee took a photo of me kissing Victor Noir and I can tell you I was satisfied, it felt quite real and I had a tingly, relaxed manner afterwards – won't need a man's lips for a few months now that I'd been with Victor.
The next day we drove out to Epernay, the capital of the Champagne region and decided to stop there for the night because there was a municipal swimming pool nearby where we could hopefully have a proper shower in the morning. Lo and behold, as we arrived, there was an obnoxious Australian girl mouthing off to someone in a bar. They really do get everywhere. By now, we really were enjoying sleeping in the car. It's okay once you get the hang of it and the monetary benefits speak for themselves. We had a rotation system because of the four possibilities: the two rear seats are the same comfort-wise, the passenger seat is the

cream of the sleeping places and the driver's seat is the worst horror of all because of the steering wheel banging on your knees. Sark drew a diagram of sleeping positions in her diary. We all sat in there before sleeping, merrily puffing away with the windows closed to keep us warm, playing cards, chatting and listening to tapes. Smoking was banned first thing in the morning as all of us (apart from Sark) were people that smoked after 11am at least. Sark was a first-thing-in-the-morning type and so we had forbidden her to light up unless she was prepared to stand outside in the cold. She wasn't a morning person and was prone to have black moods which we called her 'blackies', which could be terrifying. The sodding swimming pool was fermée but we used the toilets in the civic centre for dishwashing and bodily hygiene. A tube of wet-ones acted as washing-up facilities and we would wipe the cutlery down with them but now and again we liked to give all the utensils a proper wash with fairy liquid in hot water. We discovered rectangular shaped crackers which provided a bit of respite from baguettes and we created what we referred to as Scooby Snacks - layers upon layers of these crackers with the obligatory triangle cheese, jam, peanut butter and marmite the latter two of which were on their last scrapings and we couldn't find any similar substitute in the French supermarkets.

Today we pootled around the Champagne region admiring the landscape when we spotted a glorious sight in the distance:

"Is that what I think it is?" said Flee

"Dunno, I can't read the sign from here," I said.

"It looks like a leisure centre!" declared Flee.

And indeed it was. There perched on a hill, in all its red-bricked glory, was a leisure centre. We swung dramatically into the next available exit and raced up to the entrance. A group of school kids were having swimming lessons so we waited for the reception to be clear and edged commando-style past any danger spots into the female changing rooms. Oh for hot showers and washed hair! With heavenly, clean and soap-scented bodies, with hair shining like a VO5 advert, we had to literally hot-foot it out for fear of getting caught. As we drove away and got back on the open road we were passed by a car full of men pointing and waving at us so we all waved back with smiles on our faces. A closer look however, revealed they were concerned and pointing at the back of our car. We finally discerned that petrol was leaking out of our petrol cap when we went round a roundabout (quelle horreur!) so we stopped the car and checked it out. It all seemed to be in place but we had just filled the tank up so maybe that was why, we were not really sure. The car was a bit basic and quite old and we decided to call the RAC people after we dropped Yumi off.

Yumi's last night started off with us drinking two bottles of wine in the car, singing along at the top of our voices to a James Brown tape, dancing in the car to

Deep Heat 4 and then crashing into the nearest bar in a town called Soissons. There is actually a town in the Champagne region called Bouzy which we found rather amusing. In our drunken stupor we had some interesting conversations with Yumi. She discovered to our amazement and her surprise that gay men had anal sex and on that same subject Yumi told us that if you massage your feet regularly it is good for your health and in the morning you will have "one golden shit". The next day we headed back to Paris and Charles de Gaulle airport stopping off at an old windmill along the way. Yumi shed a few tears at the airport. It was depressing to see her go, knowing that she had to go back to school, and work, and her landlord.
"Sad to see Yumi go, it's been an intense few weeks" I said.
"Look on the bright side Beck," said Flee "No one will have to sleep in the driver's seat anymore."
Flee had a point. Every cloud has a silver lining and that afternoon we struck gold in Neuilly near Bois de Boulogne, a haven of trannies and persons seeking group sex according to Marilyn. In the course of our usual wanderings and window-shopping forays, we took the scenic route down a little side street and found a funny little delicatessen. We ventured in because it looked interesting. Flee was at the end of one of the aisles holding up a small tin in front of her.
"Is this what I think it is?" said Flee.
"It can't be!" from Sark.
"No, it's some weird vegan food, it'll be all dry and crunchy and that," I said.
"I don't think it is Beck, get out the dictionary," Flee suggested
The tin said Beurre de cacahuètes so we thumbed open the dictionary and scanned through 'B'.
"Quick, look, it's there, it's there!" we all squealed.
We had found Peanut Butter at last.
"It still might not be the actual stuff like we have, it may be a vile French version," I warned.
"It's 1 franc, let's chance it," said Flee dryly.
It was exactly like the real thing, even though it was in a tin and needed to be opened with a tin-opener. Dining was going to be better from now on. For the rest of that afternoon we killed-time in Pigalle. We could think of a lot worse places to kill time and we soaked up the true, clichéd, Parisian atmosphere outside the Moulin Rouge, with lots of sex shops, and cinemas, much like Soho but accompanied by accordionists. After this brush with heterosexuality, we balanced things out with a wander around Le Marais, the gay area and then onto Bastille where we encountered a mad screaming man on the metro; much prefer the accordionists.
Our last night in Paris and "Gay Black Lionel" as we started to call him, turned

out to be a real gem. He kept us going by being a wonderful host and tour guide and took us to Montmarte, Sacre Coeur and tonight he treated us three to a meal, in a typical old fashioned French restaurant, in Montparnasse, with red & white check tablecloths. Frisée salad with baked goat's cheese & bacon to start, followed by steak and chips (the first time I had eaten a steak in my life), a cheese course and tarte tatin for dessert. A fitting end to our time in gay (Black Lionel) Paris!

Chapter Five
Sylvain, Pat & Luc

We spent the night in Antony and called the RAC the next day. Turns out there was a hole in the pipe just under the petrol cap so that when the tank was full and we went round a corner, some overflow petrol would dribble out. The mechanic got a big piece of rubber and jubilee-clipped it around the hole to fix the problem and off we went heading south. Our song of the moment was King of the Road and Sark sang The Proclaimers-style with a heavy Scottish accent and we all joined in loudly with "I Ain't Got No Cigarettes!"

Dijon of mustard fame is a wondrous mediaeval town decked out in mustard and pink, exquisite architecture with roof tops to die for. Flee was going roof mad, she's got a thing about them; I'm quite partial to them myself. It was also cake heaven and we all realised our favourites - mine a mille-feuille (like a custard slice but better) and Flee and Sark were wobbly flan girls which were too boring for me - I need a bit of variety of textures in my patisserie. We found a new home in the open central car park which was free and near a suitable bar called Le Club for washing. Dijon, in fact, had a public swimming pool nearby which we walked to one evening, swam in and then had a proper shower. We went to into a bar called Pub Brighton because we thought it might be interesting (never go by names!) and the only interesting thing that happened was my walking through the door and knocking the cellar lid onto the waiter's head by accident and nearly killing him. We kept getting stared at, obviously looking different to the other girls. Mind you, they were a bit boring and all dressed the same in a very staid and middle-class manner; very safe. We always seemed to attract the young lads but nobody our age. Whole groups of them followed us around trying to either sell or give us disco tickets. They were all very cute but far too young. We consoled ourselves with frequenting bars that had dishy waiters as that way we could ogle at will, knowing they had no escape. One bar we went to had personal jukeboxes on each table but it was deathly quiet. Sark pressed a

couple of buttons and suddenly Rock This Town, by The Stray Cats, came blaring out. How apt! The centre was lively enough and full of students whom we were starting to interact with, using our progressing French, and their knowledge of some English or a mixture of both.
"I love the Eeengleesh music, it is the best," one spaced-out boy told us.
"Really?"
"Yes, this Eeeengleesh music is zee best!"
"What music do you like?"
"I like L'amour."
"L'amour? What, you like love songs?"
"No!!! Le Moor"
"Le Moor? What is Le Moor?"
"You know it!! Le Moor, Pink Floyd"
"Ohhhhhh. Le mur. The Wall."
"Yes, Pink Floyd, The Wall. This is the best."
We'd rediscovered chocolate spread, it was everywhere and better than that stuff from the Co-op in the '70s. We could now make out own pain au chocolat but still we thought and talked about food a lot. We went for a coffee in a fish restaurant where a beautiful man worked. (We called him Fish but he wasn't like that ugly fuck from Marillion). The downside to this was having to endure people eating oysters and moules and leaving things on their plates which I was so tempted to go by and nab or even ask for.
"Don't you dare, Beck!"
"It's such a waste of food!"
"You can't nick food from other peoples' plates!"
We liked Dijon, it felt comfortable; maybe we could get a job here in a restaurant kitchen to get free food and leftovers. I had experience in the catering trade and you don't really need to talk when you are the washer-upper. Flee had an informative booked called Work Your Way Around the World, from which she read out a chapter about staying in a nunnery in Spain. Flee was willing to pretend to be a Christian for at least one night. She'd fit in, she looks a bit like Audrey Hepburn.
That afternoon, whilst at home in Place de la République car park, smoking away, we noticed a quite handsome man, tall, slim with thick curly hair pacing up and down as if he was waiting for someone. We were analysing his appearance in a builderish manner and tried to imagine who he was waiting for. He was dressed in jeans, a denim shirt and a denim jacket, so we called him Denim. He went to the phone box, then came back, then paced around some more and then back in the phone box. I decided to wave at him. He came over to speak to us but couldn't speak English but I got by in French.

"Où vivez-vous?"(Where are you living?)
"Dans la voiture."
"Dans la voiture?"
"Oui, dans la voiture."
"Dans la voiture?"
"Oui, dans la voiture."
This mantra was to be repeated on a regular basis with everyone we met in France.
Denim seemed concerned and said we could maybe live with him and his friend and so he went and made a phone call. He returned and invited us to his house for coffee which turned out to be 40km away and we followed him there in his car, all the time wondering whether the guy was a weirdo, or not. Close up he had really pitted skin and really shaky hands. We arrived at his little village and were greeted by Armande, his woman. At first she looked a bit apprehensive (wouldn't you!) but the ice was broken by their little black kitten, Panther. After a pigeon conversation and two cups of coffee, Luc (Denim's real name), gave us his address and also that of Armande's parents in Paris. We were also given a tour of the house which was massive and empty. Luc's room was spotless and bare, everything neatly folded and spartan. We went downstairs and suddenly they told us to stay for dinner and made us take off our coats. They served us a hearty duck casserole with wine and we all sat around their telly and watched Benny Hill in French. Luc told us he was 31 and then talked about Paris and how he hated it when he lived there (his car had Parisian plates) and said it was too violent for him. Luc said he was going to try and find a job at a hotel in Dijon tomorrow and would we like to go with him. We arranged to meet him at 9.30am in our car park, kissed Luc & Armande goodbye and drove off, delighted. We couldn't believe our luck but we did ponder their generosity. That night we recorded ourselves singing a made-up song about Benny Hill. It was based on Brezairola - Berceuse by Canteloube because of the 'Bene Bene' line in that old operatic song; that was then mixed up with the show's theme tune and our lyrics 'Oh Benny, Benny, Benny, Benny Hill, you're so ugly you make me ill'. Flee was annoyed because we'd taped onto the end of one of her infamous shagging tapes. Luc didn't show up, as arranged, so we went and carried out our ablutions in the bar and left a note for him on the wind screen. We got back and he had left a return note. His car had not started. We spent the afternoon on a vineyard tour because we'd read it was free and we were hoping to get a gratis glass of wine out of it. Morin Père et fils at Nuits-Saints-Georges; where a charming stereotypical Frenchman showed us around the cellars and gave us the history of the vineyard. We were the only people there and as we were leaving I grabbed my moment and made a glass-to-the-mouth gesture. He pinched me on the cheek with a naughty

grin on his face and led us to the tasting area where we sampled (and swallowed) three types of their wine which were very nice indeed. We got back home later and who should turn up but Luc & Armande, Luc with his lovely curly hair all slicked back behind his ears, and clad in a dodgy pair of Dick Deadeye flares, with a non-matching jacket. Luc suggested I should go to the telephone with him and phone the hotel bloke to arrange a "rendezvous" and so we went over to the cabinet while Sark & Flee stayed with Armande. While Luc and I were waiting for the phone to become free, old Denim declared his love for me and said that he and Armande were 'just good friends' who lived together because of the money. He kept looking into my eyes imploringly and then asked me if I had ever been inside a prison. It was awkward. The phone became free so we went in and made the call although Luc used the opportunity to press up close to me in that bloody phone booth. We arranged to meet the hotel bloke at 4pm the next day but he only wanted one person. Luc knows of some free lodgings (free lodgings?) around the corner from our car park and agreed to take us there at 10am the following morning. That night we went to our local, Le Club, and got chatting to a semi-English speaking rotund, jewellery-clad bloke called Sylvain who was always in there propping up the bar and laughing with the manager:
"Have you seen that horrible cheap chunky bracelet he wears?" I asked
"Yeah, that silver thing with big lettering," agreed Flee
"Yeah, why on earth would you buy a silver bracelet with the word 'Silver' on it?"
"Perhaps he bought it not knowing what it meant because it's in English," said Flee
"Maybe got it in London," I said.
"You idiots, it doesn't say 'Silver' - it says Sylvain, that's his name, it's an identity bracelet!" sighed Sark
"Of course, it's upside down, thought it looked a bit odd."
Sylvain was actually a good laugh and came and sat at our table with his friend Pat who was a skinny little bald thing who looked like that bloke off Benny Hill. Sylvain was a social worker who was into hand-gliding, skiing, climbing and also jumped off bridges on big pieces of elastic, with a group of other nutters. The usual mantra about the car ensued but in English which was then translated from Sylvain to Pat with the same incredulity.
"You can all sleep at my apartment tonight" Sylvain said.
"Really!"
"Really, it is just across the car park and there is no problem, you are safe with me, nothing will happen, you don't have to be my girlfriends or anything like that."
"Okay, thanks, we'll stay then."
We later struck up a conversation with the manager's son, Manon, who spoke

perfect English with an American accent. He was a trained pilot in search for work and he told us not to worry about Sylvain and Pat, they were "good blokes". Sylvain lived in a quaint attic flat which was very French and simple. He got out his guitar and crooned us a few tunes. Pat even belted out a Jacques Brel song to my delight and we all had a sing-song and went to bed at about 3am. As I was settling down to sleep, I heard some strange friction sounds and some muffled groans. The three of us were all in a double bed, Sylvain was in another room and Pat was in a sleeping bag on the floor in the same room as us. The morning revealed our suspicions as we'd all heard the same unmistakable noises and poor old Flee was on the edge of the bed nearest to Pat. The bloke was having a wank in Sylvain's sleeping bag! Pat scurried off in shame to work and Sylvain let us all have a bath before leaving to meet Luc. How sweet he was and maybe he also had a wank over us but at least he had the decency to leave the room.

As planned we met Luc at 10am and he drove us in his car to the hostel. He greeted me with a passionate embrace as if I was his woman and from that moment on treated me as such. He was starting to get on my nerves. We stood in the foyer of the hostel and Luc asked for Monsieur Michel who appeared and scowled at us. He was young but was incredibly shady-looking with beady eyes. Luc rang a bell while Mr Shady unlocked the iron barred doors. Across the road stood three male lunch-outs who looked like they were waiting to get inside. Luc then picked up some files from his car and gave them to me with his keys and told us to wait for him because Mr Shady could not see us until 12.15pm and it was only 11am. Luc then disappeared inside for ages and we were starting to feel uncomfortable about the whole thing. I decided to chance it and rang the bell. A girl appeared at the iron gates and got Mr Shady who copped when I asked for Luc who then sheepishly appeared from a side door. I gave him his files and keys and we legged it back to our car and moved out of Place de la Republique for good. It was a shame about Luc, he didn't say much apart from tell us he had a black-belt in karate and a degree in philosophy. I felt a bit sorry for him and wished we could have spoken better French to find out more but maybe it was for the best. It was at that moment that I wondered what was happening with 'the war' as it was supposed to start today, January 15th.

Chapter Six
Our First Gibraltarian

We went for a very long coffee at Le Cabaret (Fish's bar) so we could ogle over that horny specimen for the last time before driving towards Lyon where my other pen-friend, Corrine, a member of the French dance troupe I'd met the previous summer in Moscow, lived with her brother.

We reached the city of Lyon, late, after driving through scary thick fog with only the light relief of our French radio station of choice 'Energie!' or 'NRJ' to be precise. There's a song we all liked which must have been topping the charts, by a French woman called Niagara, we saw her on MTV, bit of a goth but it was a good song 'Pendant Que Les Champs Brülent' a very sombre soundtrack to accompany the drive. We parked somewhere convenient and went to the nearest bar and, as luck would have it the girl behind the bar spoke fluent English and was really charming. She lived in a flat above the bar with her boyfriend Mike who came in later. He was tall and slim with another one of those Kevin Keegan mullets but was far more attractive than 'Fatty the Florist'. He sat down with us and started chatting away fluently in a very odd accent.

"Are you French?" We asked.
"No, I am a Gibraltarian." Mike replied.
"What's a Gibraltarian?" We barked ignorantly.
"Fuck, you're English and you don't know what a Gibraltarian is, I am British!"
"Nah ,you're not."
"I am, I'm from Gibraltar, the British colony," said Mike.
"What, the Rock of Gibraltar with the apes?" said Sark.
"Yes, the Rock of Gibraltar with the apes," Mike sighed.
"Are you a squaddie?" I enquired.
"No, I am a Gibraltarian British citizen but I live here in France now. Here, look at my passport."

Mike showed us his blue British passport with his face inside and told us the story of how he'd been living in London - Shepherd's Bush, to be exact- when he had met Vera. They had moved to France and he was a plumber by trade and had a steady job as "the plumber of the tax office". He could not believe that we lived in a car, let alone a Renault 5, and his conversation was peppered with references to our car. Mike and Vera insisted that we stay the night in their flat and have a meal with them so we gratefully obliged. We went upstairs to their alternative den, filled with ethnic decor and objects bought whilst travelling.
"Do you smoke ganga?" Mike enquired,
"Yes."
"I'm gonna get you some good shit, it has a different taste here, more flowery. They say it is not as good as London shit but this shit is far better than that London shit, it's the Algerian connection with France, they got good shit down there, like in Morocco, Morocco has very good shit"
The 'shit' was passed around and Vera and Mike were taking turns in the kitchen with the food preparation. Mike then stuck a second joint into the end of a device that was a Moroccan pipe disguised as a walking stick. Vera then passed us some lethal-looking bright green aperitifs.
"Drink!" demanded Mike.
So we did.
"Renault Cinq, shit, Renault Cinq, you English shits, I no bloody sleep in no Renault Cinq, I'd rather sleep on the street! Out on the street! You know what I mean man, do you know what I mean. Don't tell me, I know, I slept in a bloody combie with six people but no fucking Renault Cinq (belly laugh), you English. Right, I tell you what we're gonna do, we're gonna have a drink, you know what I mean man, we'll have a drink, maybe some coffee, maybe something else, some beer maybe, then we'll have a couple of joints, have a smoke then we are gonna eat something, some fish, some pasta, fromage, yaourt, because I know what it's like to be starving, don't tell me, I'm fucking starving as well you know what I mean, shit, Renault Cinq. I don't know what the food's called, eat it, if you like it you like it, if you don't you don't, Renault Cinq shit!"
Mike and Vera then led us to the dining table and we all sat down waiting for our first course. We were indeed 'fucking starving' by then so Mike told us to help ourselves to the jar of gherkins on the table. The others politely took one each but I don't know what came over me and I had one, then two, then three until I had almost polished the whole thing off; uncontrollable! The meal was fabulous and it was amazing that these strangers had invited us into their home, fed us, watered us, gave us a warm bed and got us all dog-bollock stoned. The down side of all this was we had to get up at the crack of dawn because they both had to go to work. We said our goodbyes and thank-yous and drove away only to

park up five minutes later and fall asleep. Albeit with terrible hangover, we had to admit that fate had dealt us some good cards. We spent the day discovering Lyon which was another delightful French city with rivers, bridges and well-preserved historical architecture. We walked over a footbridge across the Rhône and it gave you a weird sensation as if it was moving, which indeed it was. Sark and Flee, fascinated by this phenomenon, both jumped up and down on one end, laughing whilst I was stuck in the middle of the bridge, screaming in terror. They both heard me and stopped and then had to rescue me reeling around in a vertiginous hell. We later drove up to Basilique de Fourvière a church with lovely mosaics, on top of a hill overlooking the city. We nearly crashed into someone when coming out of the car park and we all screamed "Arrêtez Arrêtez!" out of our open windows. Sark then leaned out and with a sweep of her arm looked the driver in the eyes and said "cédez le passage!" in a really strong Dell Boy accent.

The evening brought heavy, heavy rains and there was nothing worse than rain-soaked clothes in a small car. Even if we went to a bar we would never properly dry out and trying to peel off wet jeans inside a car full of people and rucksacks was trying, to say the least. We tried to avoid getting caught out but sometimes it was impossible.

Early next morning we woke to discover the car all covered in frost, even on the inside. It was terribly cold and Sark was in a blackie so went back to sleep and woke up at 11.30am. The sun was shining but it was still freezing. We managed to get the car started after some difficulty and drove out of the car park but, just as we got to some busy traffic lights, the thing conked out. Sark and Flee got out and pushed and it started so I drove it down the hill but then it stopped again. We decided to give the RAC a call and we waited in a bar for a mechanic. We saw the headlines of two English newspapers on a stand; Saddam Hussein was not budging from Kuwait so the war was full on. The mechanic arrived and checked the car, he said the engine was fine but he thought something was wrong with the pipe connecting the petrol tank to the carburettor. That old chestnut! We waited patiently in the garage and read through the RAC gumph: if your car has to stay in for repairs overnight and you are en route to your destination they will pay for an hotel. We were not going to tell them that we lived in our car because we were sure it would make our claim null and void but if needs be we could always say we are on our way to Marseille or somewhere south and wangle a night in an hotel. At that point we looked out of the window to see two young mechanics in blue overalls speeding around the forecourt and doing 3-point turns in our car, whilst roaring with laughter. The novelty of a French car with right-hand drive obviously tickled their fancy. The car was presented to us as fixed but then promptly broke down again just as we were leaving. More sitting around in the garage waiting and shivering in the foyer, with no offer of coffee or tea. Dejected, we got out our Bumper Road Map of Europe where amongst other interesting facts the colour key showed blue-almost-white for places like Finland and then orange-almost-red for North Africa.

"Where in Europe is the reddest?" Flee asked

"Right there!" I pointed with my finger on Málaga in the south of Spain.

"That is where we are going, agreed?" Said Flee.

"Agreed. No stopping, only to sleep," I said.

"Deal!" Said Sark.

I felt much better now; I love a big decision.

On the drive back we heard Fog on the Tyne on the radio but the Gazza version which prompted us to write our own poignant version later that evening:

Fog On The Rhône (Imagine it sung by Gazza)

Sitting in a bar in Vieux Lyon
Some people sat down and said 'come on'
Let's go and have a drink over in Perrache
But I got up and had a slash

Fog on the Rhône is all mine all mine, fog on the Rhône is all mine!

Mike and Vero were really alright
Said that we could crash on their floor for the night
Got out the ganga and blew off my head
Ate their gherkins and went to bed

Fog on the Rhône is all mine all mine, fog on the Rhône is all mine!

Heard a funny noise in my old Renault Cinq
But the sound was not as bad as Pat having a wank
Took it to the garage, ate a custard slice
Licked my lips and said 'That was nice'

Fog on the Rhône is all mine all mine, fog on the Rhône is all mine!

We couldn't leave just yet as we'd agreed to meet Corrine and that would hopefully mean a decent hot meal and maybe even a bed for one night. We needed to cash some of our travellers' cheques so found a bank and went to Tourist Information in an effort to be entertained. Lyon was becoming familiar, especially Vieux Lyon, the old quarter where we decided to 'live' and hang out. That was the beauty of living in the Renault 5 - we could live in the poshest parts of town. We did a tour of the Traboules de la Croix-Rousse, dark old alleyways used for transporting precious silks to keep them out of the elements and then later used by the French Résistance to hide from the Nazis. They were intriguing, like rabbit warrens going in and out of secluded cobbled courtyards.

We hadn't washed or changed our clothes in five days. We cleaned our teeth morning and night but that was all. It was far too cold to throw water over ourselves and there was nowhere to do it properly. Our favourite haunt in Vieux Lyon was Café de la Cathédrale where we named the barman, Justin, because he looked like someone who would be called Justin; a mincer wearing paisley or heraldic-print shirts and saying "Mercibonsoir" all in one word. Later that evening we saw Justin in a rival establishment down the street - Cafe Comptoir where he was being served a delicious-looking meal by, Mimi, the husky-voiced avant-garde proprietress. We noticed that there were always hard boiled eggs on the bar in a special rack and we had seen such racks in other traditional bars in France. We saw people just help themselves as if the eggs were free but none of us ever dared. We knew that in France there was a tradition about them never charging for bread with the meal but that was slightly different because one would have bought the meal. But what about these eggs, it had said in one of our guide books that they were free but was it just an urban myth? It was torture looking at those frigging eggs but we were just too polite to do anything.

"I am bloody fed-up of coffee, hot chocolate and cigarettes. What I want is a MAN, they warm you up and they don't cost anything" Sark blurted out.

We had one of our 'what I could really do with' conversations e.g. "What I could really do with right now is..." and we'd all say something:

Mashed Potato

Chips

Curry & Rice

Cornish Pasty

Pies in any shape or form

Cauliflower Cheese

A fuck-off girt Roast Dinner

Treacle pudding with custard

Lasagne

A decent cup of tea that doesn't cost over two quid.

Flee and I had taken to eating sugar cubes neat. Neither of us took sugar in our coffee and realised we were fools to just leave the cubes behind so would bag them for some later moment when a sugar craving came upon us. Crunchy sugar cubes are divine, by the way. Later that evening, in Café de la Cathédrale, we were all delighted by a different barman who was Sting's twin but rather than partake in his juicy company we were set upon by the ugliest man in the world who made Fergal Sharkey look like Elvis. He was only about our age but looked knocking-on forty, with one tooth longer than all the rest, and a chin which curled up nearly touching his nose. He looked like the "scary moon in profile", as the nice moon 'face on' looks like Paul McCartney according to Sark. He told us he was an expressionist artist who had to stop painting because his work was too violent and it had "saturated him". Sting and Justin were laughing from the bar, along with an Adam Ant clone with pointy sideburns, which brought us all together and we finally started chatting.

"Three men, three wallets and three empty spaces at a dinner table," said Sark

"Three empty beds hopefully" added Flee.

"Let's ask them about the eggs!" I said.

Sark had earlier found a beer mat with some poetic scribblings on it, about lost love and women, signed by someone called James. A few minutes later we met a Canadian bloke called James, was it one and the same? We ended up round his flat and he presented each of us with a huge bar of chocolate and said we could stay the night. We got our sleeping bags and found a place to bed down. James told me to go into his mate's room. He was fast asleep and must have wondered who the hell I was when he got up in the morning. James was just a Canadian twat really, who was nervous, had a stutter and went on about The Lord of the Rings, past loves, played 'Stairway to Heaven' on his guitar and would gratingly stop mid-sentence and ask: "What are you thinking?" Of course I was thinking what a total arsehole he was but I just said "I was thinking it was time to go to sleep". He was kind and he did give us chocolate, plus a Let's Go Europe! guidebook (Let's Go France 88! had been invaluable to us) and he arranged his toilet-rolls in a pyramid shape on the bathroom floor which was pretty cool. In the morning he fed us and we left him there reading. He said it stopped him thinking.

Our dinner invite at Corrine's came to fruition and we found out there were public showers at Port-Dieu station for 15F but the old hag 'in yer face' toilet assistant patrolled the joint like a pro and was insistent that we went in one at a time (?) and spent the requisite 'VINGT MINUTES! VINGT MINUTES!' After a good vingt minutes wash we went to a department store and sprayed on expensive perfumes. Corrine was on top form and wearing hot pants. She was with her friend Agnes and her brother (another Laurent but this one a jerk). Corrine told us she was in love with Lionel (wasn't everybody?) We drank loads of tea, then loads of wine, I sang a song and she served up her homemade pizza followed by a regional dish of Quinelles, finishing off with cheese, yogurt and cake for dessert. We were all shocked that she smoked at the same time as eating her yoghurt. Is there no end to the Frenchness of the French?

Chapter Seven
Car Trouble

We treated ourselves to a mille-feuille and two slices of flan as this could be the last time we had the chance as we were not sure what Spanish cakes were like. We packed up the car and set off towards Andorra and a lovely long and sometimes hair-raising drive through snowy mountains. As we passed Le Puy, we saw a massive pink statue of Madonna & Child on top of a hill. The drive was long but beautiful with everything under a blanket of snow and we reached Toulouse at midday with 'NRJ' keeping us entertained along the way. The Undertones tape started to slow down and Fergal went from a baritone to a bass. Batteries needed replacing so French radio it was, although Roxette was starting to get on our nerves and we would have to tune into some other more palatable station. We did the usual bank and coffee stop and started up again but the car just stopped. We'd run out of petrol again but something must be wrong as we had a quarter of a tank. Flee and I pushed the car, embarrassingly, along a main road and then parked it in a nice spot by a canal and headed off to the petrol station with an empty canister. We poured some petrol in but the car would still not go. Two young boys and an old man tried to help and told us our ignition was faulty and that the car could not start because petrol was getting into the carburettor. We decided it was time to hassle the RAC as the car had never really been fixed since the beginning and we needed it sorted. We told them we were en route to stay with friends in Spain and needed to be given accommodation while our car got properly fixed. The brow-beating worked, they telexed through the money and we spent the next half an hour discussing how many hours each of us would spend in the bath. The car got fixed by the evening so we drove it to our posh Hotel Ibis and swanned into the reception to collect our keys. Complete and utter bliss, a room with three clean beds, with crisp white sheets and unlimited hot water. We all had baths, pedicures, manicures, shaved off a lot of hair and then went down to the bar for a celebratory drink which was only slightly marred by some English blokes talking loudly about how many hours "Mark from Chester" took to get drunk. In the morning I had another shower and washed my hair again, it was such a novelty. We ate like pigs from the breakfast buffet. Mr Sage Suit, the hotel manager, came and asked if we were okay and a Bill Wyman look-alike stared at us. We managed to shake both of them off and surreptitiously return to the buffet for more croissants which we then shoved in a bag and took back to the room for later. Gotta get it while you can! We spent the morning in the room watching telly and I wrote a letter to Yumi and my old boyfriend Mark (not "Mark from Chester"). We considered trashing our hotel room like rock stars but just nicked an ashtray and left a couple of dirty rings around the bath. We set off in the direction of Spain, through the snow-capped Pyrenees, which led us up to Andorra. It truly was breathtaking. At a high point we stopped the car and just got out and enjoyed the high altitude and the silence. Who was it that said we came at the wrong time of year? We got to the frontier and followed the signs through the 'city' towards Spain, we just wanted to get down south and to the sun so did not bother to stop; it looked like one big ski resort anyway and was probably really expensive. We got through customs at the other side and within minutes the whole landscape changed dramatically. We were now surrounded on both sides by steep, red, rocky mountains and there were lemon and orange trees everywhere, right by the side of the road which you could just go and pick. We had finally reached Spain.

We arrived in the town of Lleida and it was late and we were desperate for a hot drink but realised we had no pesetas. Bum. No banks would be open and all we had on us was a 50 Franc note. We walked around for ages trying to find a hotel that changed money and in our tired state we also had to get out the Spanish phrase book and ask for change in that language. Lleida is in Catalunya and signs were in Spanish and Catalan. We hadn't a clue how to speak either language and our guide book warned of the political differences in this region but we guessed that the locals would forgive us our regional ignorance if we stood in front of them, phrasebook-in-hand trying to read out a sentence. We crossed a bridge on foot and found a large hotel, went into the lobby and tried to ask to change money and were met with blank, impatient stares. In the end we just showed the receptionist the line in our book and eventually got understood, gave her our 50 Franc note and got about 1000 pesetas to spend. It was really late by now and we needed a hot drink. We walked back over the bridge and into the small town centre, found a bar and ordered three hot chocolates. What they brought us was not normal hot chocolate but more like chocolate custard in a cup, which Flee and Sark loved, but which I found a bit too sickly and thick. We now realised that chocolate was this thick stuff and Cola Cao is the normal stuff. You live and learn. We parked up to sleep in a village which was redolent of a set in a spaghetti western, expecting old Clint to walk out of the station bar at any moment. It was all so...Spanish. It was winter but everything seemed dusty and dry and a donkey tied to a railing outside a low-rise, flat-roofed white building just added to the essence.

We still had French produce in our food bag and every time we tried to speak Spanish it came out as French. We desperately wanted to see the sea so got on the road and headed for the coast towards Tarragona. How wonderful to see the clear blue of the Mediterranean and breath in its fresh smell, not like Portsmouth Harbour at all and the pebbly 'beach' at Southsea with that ever-present oily, rusty smell mixed with hot dogs and candy floss on Clarence Pier. This sea smelt of salt and fish and sand. We tuned our radio into a Spanish music channel. How were we ever going to learn this language, they spoke so bloody fast. Next stop Valencia, the third-largest city in Spain.

If it had been summer we could have experienced La Tomatina, an annual tomato fight which would have been a right laugh which perhaps we could do on the way back up to France. We had purposely missed out Barcelona as we just wanted to get to somewhere warm by the sea as quickly as possible and also earn a bit of money. We were saving Barcelona for later...We drove around the city of Valencia, taking in some majestic buildings, and got down onto the Paseo Marítimo, a three-mile-long palm tree-lined promenade where we parked up. We found the liveliest bar and tried our first tapas which were delicious and dirtiest cheap; small plates of Paella packed with seafood and fried calamares, all washed down with Rioja. We spent the whole evening in that one bar/restaurant because the atmosphere was so good but nobody spoke to us. We were all a bit pissed so probably could have had a bash at speaking Spanish with the locals without feeling silly. We walked back to the car which was parked up by a beach and slept soundly with bellies full of good food.

We set off again in the morning, first stopping off at Pryca supermarket. The food was much cheaper in Spain but now we had a whole new lot of products to decipher and still no Marmite. The cakes in Spain didn't look anywhere near as appetising as our French favourites so we avoided them, didn't want to waste our money on something that may have tasted horrible. They looked either boring and dry or overly sweet and synthetic. The tomatoes on the other hand were great big things which were a meal in themselves and sprinkled with a bit of salt and eaten like an apple went down a real treat. It was always raining but warmer than before and we could sit outside and catch some sun between the showers. Spanish towns are very pretty, even in the winter rain; tiled fronts and doorways of houses, wrought iron, shutters, blinds and balconies; orange groves, red mountains, dust, dry river beds. There was a lot of graffiti on the road signs with the Castilian crossed out replaced with Catalan. We also noticed a lot of anti Gulf War posters and graffiti in Spain and in France too. 'NO WAR' is easy to decipher in any country. The roadworks sign is much the same as the UK one i.e. a red triangle with a man bending down shovelling up earth, but the Spanish 'man' had a cool quiff hairstyle and looked like my Dad so whenever we passed one they shouted out "Alright Dave!"

Benidorm was a place that we really wanted to avoid but somehow it just drew us in and we couldn't resist a sneaky-peek at a proper naff old tourist destination. It was truly hideous, with the dodgiest postcards ever put into print, so awful that we had to buy a load and send them to people. Tacky hotels, neon-lit bars, pissed-up old people everywhere and nearly all of the signs were written in English: Fish & Chips, English Sky News Here, Draught Guinness, Union Jacks, Full English Breakfast, Milky Tea. If you can't beat them join them, so we went into one of these dreadful places and bought a cup of tea for the equivalent of 25p and it was a proper mug of tea which tasted as it should do. The clientele were English and loud, men with pints in their hands and bellies hanging out from under shirts that were far too tight. They all had their chairs turned towards a telly on the wall which was blasting out Sky News and 'The War' - in fact it was entitled 'GULF NEWS' in giant lettering. We got out of there and went to find a quieter place to eat something. We figured that we might as well eat out here because it was so cheap and we knew exactly what we were getting. Minutes later we were wolfing down pasty, chips, brown sauce and beans at Taff's Bar and got chatting to a 38 year old Dutch bloke called Rop who was the only other person in there (those Dutch again!). Rop was good fun and we spent the evening in Taff's Bar, hearing his stories about the time he lived in Montmarte and was a portrait artist. He shared a flat with an insane Jewish friend called, Bernard who insisted on playing recordings of Hitler's speeches at the Nuremburg rallies. He would play them loudly, over and over and goose-step around their flat and then pretend to kill himself with a giant sword.

You can never tire of driving along the Mediterranean, everything is open and clear and blue; the sea looked so inviting although it was still far too cold to go in. Alicante was a great town, a far cry from that freak-show in Benidorm so we agreed to stop a while and take it all in. We parked in the Centro Ciudad and found Tourist Information before walking up a steep tower of steps to the foot of the old castle, by-passing typically Spanish streets covered with coloured plant pots on the walls and in the patios. We could see inside some of these houses and into their kitchens where old fat women in Hilda Ogden aprons were cooking. It was suddenly so warm!

We spent that afternoon driving up in the mountain wilderness ("Alright Dave!") behind the town and stopped in a picnic area to make a cup of tea and have a Scooby snack. In the evening we went back into the town centre which was full of youths driving around on mopeds without helmets. Alicante was buzzing and we consulted our new Let's Go Europe book for some tips on what was hot and what was not and found that the only review was: 'Gay men will enjoy the Viking Club' so we didn't bother with that one. We ended up in Bar Asia, getting high on second-hand dope smoke generously provided by the group of people sitting behind us. Spanish toilets were different to the French ones, no sit-up-and-begs here but they all had signs saying 'Don't put any paper down the toilet' and there would be bins next to the toilet bowl full of ghastly used toilet paper. Do they have something wrong with their sewage systems?

Washing needed to be done and we managed to find a launderette and washed all our clothes, apart from what we had on. That day we went to the best art gallery we'd been to so far (that included the Louvre) and it was free; the 20th Century Art Museum: Picasso; Miró; Dalí; Oldemburg; Max Ernst and Alexander Calder, plus a bonus felt-tip doodle by Jean Cocteau, and stuff by lots of other Spanish artists. This suitably inspired us so we then took the lift right to the top of Castillo Santa Barbara for 200 pesetas and gazed out for miles into the blue. That was far too much culture for one morning so we nipped into McDonalds to buy some chips and the girls in there laughed at my sunglasses.

Everyone wore coloured jeans so we went into some shops and tried them on to see how they looked. Unlike Joe Orton, cheap clothes didn't 'suit us' and the Levis looked the best so we forgot about the jeans and made do with what we had, which we were getting rather bored of by now. We drove out to Murcia through orchard after orchard, orange trees abundant and the smells were delicious and the blossom so perfumed. I love apple blossom but these orange trees were something else. The steppes were covered in olive trees and looked like Van Gogh paintings and you could see where Vincent got his inspiration. They were beautiful even when bare; maybe even more so.

Cathedrals in Spain are resplendent, gothic affairs, camp even; painful depictions of1 Christ and his wounds and the ever-present Mary always calm and serene in her blue robes, so different from England with its stark, modern Catholic churches which I had only ever seen from the outside. Palm trees were everywhere, not just along the promenades but all over the city centres and between all the buildings and lining the squares. Murcia town hall with its bright pink stucco and classical pillars was grand and glorious, worthy of being painted no doubt but it was getting dark and we needed a drink. We walked around the side streets and Sark suddenly jumped up in the air and picked a large orange from a tree "because I can" she said. We later stopped in a bar when there was a power cut the moment we sat down. The owner served us up three beers on the house and when the power came back on so did the music. He'd been playing the Gun album 'Taking on the World' from start to finish, in a tiny bar in a tiny

town. We could not believe it.
Granada was going to be our next stop; we had slept the night just outside Murcia centre and had noticed rows and rows of large posters, advertising art exhibitions and bullfights. These had already happened so we figured it would be okay to peel off a poster as a souvenir. We made sure that nobody was around and went for the ones that looked the loosest, scraped them off with our fingers and rolled them up. We headed out of there very pleased with our booty.
Car trouble again. Seems those French mechanics don't know how to fix their own cars. This time it wouldn't start and it had a flat tyre so I went to a phone box and called the RAC. If it were simply a case of changing a tyre we could have done it ourselves. After a lot of hanging around we ended up in La Jijoneca Bar in Alhama de Murcia waiting on mechanics...again. The barman was very hospitable and gave us a round of free drinks, after which a mysterious Humphrey Bogart look-alike came and picked us up and drove us to Totana where we were greeted by an obese old Spaniard Rafael who 'mañana'd' us with matter-of-fact hand gestures and said he needed a siesta before working on the car. We were then introduced to 'The Interpreter' who was young, blonde and French. He attempted to have a car conversation with us which failed and then he took us back to his bar, dumped us there and went home to have his lunch. The town didn't seem to have any women in it and we were the local novelty, it seemed, and were soon attracting the attention of male gawpers. In the bar we had what can only be described as a sardine samosa which was very good and a glass of water and were also treated to a cup of coffee and offered fags by the strangers in the bar. We found out later that old Frenchy was 21 and owned the bar (not sure how credible that info was though). His name was Sergio and he employed his swarthy young friend, Carlos, to help him out. Sergio was a flirt and a bit of a wheeler-dealer and was constantly hopping in and out of the bar or leaning into the windows of various cars that pulled up outside.
Time was really dragging and nothing was happening so we got out our deck of cards and started to play. A few weeks back in a moment of boredom, Sark had drawn a cartoon of Lemmy from Motorhead onto the Ace of Spades card which meant that whenever you got that card in your hand you couldn't help it but start sniggering and keeping a poker face was impossible but it did spice things up a bit. Us playing cards at our table attracted the attention of Mr Mad Orange Jumper who was over sixty at the very least and was curious as to what we were doing. He told us we could all go and stay in his house and also have dinner there, and he showed Sark a picture of Jesus he carried in his wallet, as verification of his honourable intentions we presumed. We never thought for a moment that we'd not be safe in his hands, but did wonder what his wife would do if we all pitched up at his place. Hours had passed and still no sign of Humphrey Bogart

or any other mechanics. We looked over to Sergio and he simply shrugged. The only upside was that we didn't pay for anything. Another sweet little old man came and sat with us and watched the game and yet more hours passed. More shrugs, more visits to the toilet, more frustration. We'd been sitting around that table for nearly six hours, on uncomfortable chairs, and being watched by all and sundry who entered the bar. One bloke had been in there longer than we had and he'd sat there in silence almost the whole time and a really annoying loud one kept coming in and out, and in and out, in and out; he looked like Dirty Den off Eastenders. Two goons from the bar thought that they would come over and show us a 'funny' mechanical key-ring which at the touch of a button depicted two pigs having sex. They'd spent most of the evening laughing hysterically over this and we had wondered what all the fuss was about - mystery solved. We caught up with our diaries, we squared each other with any monies owing (we did this every night right down to the last centime) we doodled and drew pictures and at one point Sark pushed a folded piece of paper over the table towards me which I opened and read:

Totana, Spain, 30th Jan 1991 10.30pm

Dear Beck

I am sitting near you and have been for the last 8 hours. I am very bored and will soon cut my nose off for something to do. I am sick & tired of being stared at by smarmy twats & mad men in orange jumpers. If I don't get to a hotel soon & wash my hair it will slide out of its own roots because they are so well greased. Also if the Carburetter or however you spell it breaks down again I will find a mad dog & stuff it up its arse. The tiles in front of me have turned into dancing men and I am fed up of staring at the remains of that octopus on the table. If Dennis Watts walks in again I am going to organise his assassination, it will be a slow painful death involving daffodils and a canal.

Thank you

With hair-tearing boredom

Sark x

Sergio and Carlos kept providing drinks, then food, then a lethal, spruced-up liqueur. Finally, after eight hours of waiting, old Rafael the mechanic waddled by and told us that we could drive the car, so we gathered our stuff, waved goodbye to everyone and got into the car, relieved to be getting out of there. 100 metres down the street and it stopped. Raphael slapped his forehead with his palm as he remembered that he'd only fixed the wheel but not the carburettor. Por Dios! Back into the bar we all went and I called the RAC and pulled the old 'en route to a mate's house far away' routine which worked. It was 11pm by the time we reached the hotel. I had my own room with en suite and Sierra Nevada views, and Flee & Sark shared a room. Sergio and Carlos had invited us back to their bar for drinks but Sark declined; she was tired and eventually puked up octopus tentacles in the loo. When Flee and I returned to the bar it was miraculously empty save Sergio and Carlos who had pulled down the rolling shutter almost to the floor of the entrance. Moments later we heard a knock and a man's voice, we couldn't see his face only his feet. Whoever it was got told to go away and Flee and I soon realised that we'd all been paired off and those shoes under the door belonged to a third man whom they'd lined up for Sark. After a stiff drink Sergio and Carlos pulled straws in front of us (yep, it's true, they actually did pull straws in front of us) and within moments I was on the floor behind the bar snogging Sergio and Flee was in the kitchen eating a sardine samosa with Carlos. As soon as she'd taken the last mouthful he pounced on her and proceeded to furtively grope her. I pushed Sergio off me as I could hear Flee calling out my name and Sergio went and got Carlos and told him to sit down on a chair. He obeyed and then we left. It was all pretty harmless stuff, nothing we couldn't handle and the next morning we got served a hearty breakfast by Spanish bull-women and Sark was cheered up by the story of the mystery feet:

"Better not have belonged to Dennis Watts," she said.

The car was nearly ready but we still ended up back at the bar, waiting a further two hours. To Flee's relief, Carlos had a day off and was absent so we relaxed outside in the sun and Sergio treated us to a coke. We laughed with him about Carlos or l'animal as we now called him and Sergio said "sorry about him but he's only sixteen and got over-excited". Only sixteen?!

By the time we reached Granada the car was playing up again. Was there no end to this? Tedious as it was, the car trouble was giving us more leverage with the RAC and I was starting to develop a relationship with the woman on the other end of the line. We didn't see anything of Granada, not the Alhambra, not the old town, nada. The one bit of excitement involved us all limbo-dancing in a panic under the slowly-lowering shutters of a bar as the owner tried to lock us in there with his mates. We ran down the street screaming, got into the car and sped away. Our Spanish guidebook said that 'Spanish men think that women who travel alone are looking for sexual adventure'; only the puke ones believe this it seems…

The car was still dodgy, so much for those so-called mechanics. We managed to get to a small town outside Granada called Maracena. It was pissing down with rain and there was no point in stopping, nothing looked appealing. Our car was useless in cities as it stalled at low speeds so when we reached Malaga we immediately turned left towards Nerja. The girls at Flee's work went there on holiday; it was fashionable apparently. We reached Torre del Mar on the Costa del Sol and it was pouring with rain. We needed to stop for coffee and the loo and when we got back behind the wheel the car wouldn't start. We managed to drag some boys out of an amusement arcade to help us push, no joy, so we called the RAC and got a hotel for the night. This one was grotty, no breakfast included and in the morning. Sark looked like an Old English Sheepdog because she'd gone to bed with wet hair. The RAC said we'd be transported to Gibraltar by truck that morning so we waited for said truck in a cafe and an hour later two Neanderthal slobs turned up but insisted they had a coffee first. They then told us that only one of us could travel in the truck to Gibraltar and the other two had to catch a bus or taxi, no way! More rants on the phone to the RAC and we were back in the bar, waiting, sitting next to a fruit machine that played La Cucaracha over and over. Slob No1 was supposed to return in 15 minutes but quelle surprise he didn't. When he finally made an appearance he had brought along the Norman Wisdom of Spain to act as interpreter and told us the car would be "ready soon". Much, much later Slob No 2 returned and- wait for it- explained that "there is a hole in the petrol pipe which is letting water into the petrol tank causing disruption to the carburettor". If that frigging French twat in Antony had properly welded the pipe, instead of wrapping a bit of rubber round it, we would never have had all these problems!

By this time the slobs had developed a rapport with us and took us to their local while the car was being finished off and when I was alone with one of them he asked me out on a date, adding that he had a couple of mates for Sark & Flee. What was it with Spanish old men? He was way over fifty and not the most attractive specimen; beer gut, black teeth, grey brylcremed hair – say no more. Sark who test-drove the car with one of them, accidentally rubbed her hand up his leg instead of the gear stick which he took to mean something else. Yet again we made another farcical quick escape under duress; it really was becoming tiring. This much attention would be annoying even from a bevy of Adonises when you're just trying to get your car fixed and move on. To cap it all Sark crashed the car into the bumper of a family vehicle in front of her at a junction. Fortunately, they just got out, smiled, looked at their damage and said "No Problem". Our Renault 5 was unscathed.

Chapter Eight
Ronda

Sark's parents, along with her Auntie Sharyn & Uncle Bryan (both spelt with a Y), were coming on holiday to nearby Estepona at the end of February and we figured that they'd allow us at least one nights' kip in their golf villa. So with that utopia in mind we thought we'd start to explore the area and get to know Spain. Just a short drive through the ghastly Puerto Banus had us running for the hills. Yet again another clone-town full of English posers and other pretentious jerks. We left England to get away from these bastards!

"Drive away now, get away from this place" Flee begged.

So we did indeed head for the hills and drove round hairpin bends and along cliff edges ("Alright Dave!"). It was getting late and the brick red mountains were now covered in a blood-red sunset. It was awesome scenery. Soon it would be dark and we kept on driving up and up. In the distance we saw something twinkling and as we got closer noticed it was a pretty white city on the top of a mountain beckoning us forth.

Ronda is situated on a pinnacle 750m high and all around the town are sheer cliff drops with panoramic views. It was ancient, well preserved and full of stunning architecture, including the oldest bullring in Spain. We fell in love instantaneously and found a free car park right outside the Cathedral, in a square full of orange trees in full abundance. It was a lovely spot until we noticed uniformed men going in and out of one of the buildings and realised we'd parked up in front of the bloody cop-shop so swiftly moved on. Sleeping in the car was second-nature to us now and the jackpot position was the area behind the driver's seat because that could now be pushed forward over the steering wheel, leaving lots of leg room. With a full rucksack wedged underneath it almost created a bed.

The worst thing was having your period and waking up in the morning with nowhere to flush a tampon away and not enough time to get to a bar. We'd all have our morning piss in the street beside the car if desperate but the tampon

thing provided a challenge; I then discovered the art of whipping them out quickly and then catapulting it in the style of a hammer-throw over the fence and into a field of long grass. How handy were those wet-wipes!
Spanish supermarkets had some great stuff in them and all really cheap. The stationery section was the best, with lovely notebooks and pens, and Flee and Sark found proper sketch pads for 48 pesetas each; that is shockingly barato. We felt at home in Ronda and soon became quite familiar with its streets and bars, our favourite being Café Cristina where we developed a penchant for tall glasses of hot milk which we would stir sugar into. Another was la Ibense, the ice-cream parlour. We'd spend sunny days sketching local monuments and buildings and rainy days in the Cathedrals and in the library, looking at children's books. There was a tall, dark (and not unhandsome) local loon who would sit outside the Cathedral and watch us sketch. He had a large dog and every so often would just say "Sol, Cathedral" and we would just look up at him and nod and he'd just go ahead and say it again. Ronda was full of tantalising shoe shops and little booths selling antiques and rural paraphernalia. Flee and I simply had to splash-out and buy a new pair, we were fed up with what we were wearing and needed a change, plus they were a bargain. We also bought a small cow-bell each with a piece of leather thong to hang them around our necks as musical pendants although that novelty wore off after a while with the constant tinkling and chest-banging.
Home was now 'Brighton' - a new estate which was architecturally similar to an 18th Century Brighton beach crescent. We parked up alongside the residents' cars and spent the next three weeks in the same spot without any bother. Each morning the 'parks & gardens' blokes would stare at us and gradually the stares turned into 'holas' until eventually they had their Renault 5 Baptism and had to push the car when it wouldn't start. Sark was talking in her sleep one night and saying "Si Si, No, No" and some other Spanish words so Flee and I teased her about having racy dreams involving gardeners in their blue overalls.
Using Ronda as our base we would drive out to all the white villages that were dotted around the area, our car always attracting curiosity from the locals. These little villages were so well kept, tiny shuttered windows and flowers in bloom hanging from window boxes. The streets were so narrow and it wasn't always obvious what were pedestrian areas and actual roads. In Olvera we got stuck up a steep lane that just narrowed and narrowed until it became a path which we then had to negotiate reversing down on. It was all a bit hairy but luckily we didn't scrape anything or smash off our mirrors.
Ronda itself had lots of sights and tourist attractions; the main bridge was famous during the Spanish Civil War as priests would be thrown off it into the gorge way down below, horrifying! Ronda is where modern bullfighting began and its 18th Century bullring also has a museum. This was something we didn't

mind paying for and it wasn't that expensive to get in and it gave us a chance to actually stand in the middle of the ring and walk behind the wooden guard boards around the edges. We stayed there for a couple of hours and sat in the seats under the lovely stone arches sketching them. I thought it was romantic but the others hated the place. Not sure what I would feel about seeing an actual bullfight. It would have been lovely to have somewhere proper to sleep but the Spaniards were not like the French, they were far more old fashioned and lived with their parents until they were married, in many cases, so no chance of meeting up with people our age and being allowed to sleep on their floors. We found a gem of a bar with a roaring log fire just out in the sticks which had a sink in the bathroom where you could fit your head under the tap and wash your hair. We all had long hair which we had to quickly bundle up in a clip as we couldn't really sit there in the bar with dripping locks. We necked our coffees and drove around the countryside with the windows open, drying our hair. On one such drive we were overtaken by a truck load of young soldiers who were all waving at us from the back. This happened often and we weren't sure if it was the same one truck or there were hundreds of them.

"We need to find out where they go at night," said Sark.

"Probably locked up in barracks." said Flee.

"They must be let out at some point surely?" I replied desperately.

Each evening we would go from bar to bar trying to find something to do but all the young people were paired off or were just teenagers. Packs of girls huddled in the corner of Cristina would throw us unfriendly glares. Anyone near our age was married and having family dinners in civilised restaurants. Then one night we noticed people queuing up outside a doorway down a side street, the sign above read Disco-Bar El Rocio. We followed them in and down some steps into a veritable Garden of Eden. Hallelujah, we'd found the lost island of pleasure at last. The place was jam-packed with wall-to-wall beautiful young men, and some girls too, but these paled into insignificance amidst the testosterone haze that thus engulfed us. Half an hour later, drinks downed, we were all on the dance floor 'bumping bums' with these snake-hipped beauties. However at 10.45pm they all departed in an instant, leaving the dregs and the girls in their wake. Where were they going? Did they actually exist? Was it a mirage on our part due to a long absence of suitable nubile company? We couldn't let them get away so we followed close behind undetected until we reached Plaza del Socorro where they were all bundled onto army trucks and driven away. The illusive soldiers had been located.

Every night thereafter we were boogieing on the El Rocio dance floor and by day two I'd already bagged myself a handsome soldier, Giuseppe, who was not in fact Spanish but Italian. They were all doing their National Service so weren't 'real'

soldiers which made them even more attractive in our eyes as some of them were university students with artistic tendencies and an ability to converse in English. They told us that they ran for 14 hours with heavy rucksacks on their backs, up hills; they skied, they dived, they abseiled and parachuted (all soldiers whatever their nationality say this sort of shit don't they). Giuseppe was leaving the next day so we made the most of it by kissing at every given opportunity, in the disco, in bars, under trees, in shop doorways. He was a bloody good kisser and it was sad to see him go.
"Plenty more where he came from Beck," said the girls as they kindly consoled me.
And indeed there were. Flee had locked lips with a dishy Spaniard on day two, didn't bother to ask his name but was now mesmerised by a new interest whom we christened 'Sexy Bum' because it was his stand-out quality. He had a friend who was equally beautiful but not with the same posterior so he got called 'Ugly Bum'. These two were often holding court with a group of swooning local girls, strutting their stuff on the dance floor while the females just sat there all coy.
There was no time to lose so we braved the floor and soon I was getting swung around by 'Ugly Bum' and being sung to in Spanish much to the displeasure of the on-looking girls. In the ensuing days we got to know them all and learned that 'Ugly Bum' was called Juan and 'Sexy Bum', Jesus.
"Jesus? That's not your real name?" We asked.
"It is!" Said Jesus.
"You can't be called Jesus, nobody calls their kid Jesus," We said.
"Si, si. Look at my ID".
It was true. Jesus was alive and well and living in Ronda with a very sexy bum. Flee had finally come to love and worship Jesus. Maybe we should go and look for that convent after all…
Last year, my American cousin, Kathy, had travelled round Europe in a proper camper van (they're Americans, of course they'd travel in a proper vehicle!) and she told me that one day, the four of them decided to spend a day alone and meet up in the evening to 'share and discuss' what they had all done. We decided to do the same and so we parted one morning and I headed down to the river and the old bridges with a sketch pad and pencils (those darn artists were influencing me). I wandered around the old Arabic quarter which had some derelict Moorish baths and was flanked by a shanty town full of chickens, the odd horse and corrugated iron sheeting a-plenty. Squalor beside beauty, so Ronda did have a dark side then. Elvis Costello was keeping me company on my walkman and I stopped and bought a can of beer from a kiosk and some 10p mix-up sweets. After I had my lunch by the river I walked up and found a market in a square and some cheap jeans caught my eye. I went with the stall-holder woman to a nearby

bar toilet in order to try them on. It was very cold and had started to snow a bit so I was wearing my Russian hat which was attracting stares from people. One little boy fell off his bike as he stopped to gawp in wonder. It was really odd being away from the others and because we did not have any money, we couldn't do anything that exciting apart from wander around streets we had not been down before.

Later I met up with the others and exchanged stories. Sark had been to the circus tent in the fair and then witnessed a house fire and the whole street was in a panic, with the fire brigade trying to squeeze down a narrow lane. She'd also been to a cafe and written letters. Flee immersed herself in her music and her roofs and spent the day sketching and painted the beautiful roofs of Ronda, having herself a little picnic and dreaming about Jesus and his bright, white underpants poking out from under his jeans.

We had a night with the lads as usual, and Sark was feeling a bit peaky so Jesus gave her some pills to take which she swallowed down with her drink! We drove them all back to camp and who was on guard duty outside, but Ugly Bum, Juan, who cut a fine figure in his uniform and gun? Despite his intentions at being serious, he allowed us to touch his live weaponry. We finished off our evening in the 'hair washing bar' and passed the football stadium along the way. Ten minutes later the bar was wall-to-wall with trumpet-blowing, flag-waving happy men singing 'Ole Ole Ole Ole'; they must have won the match.

Sark had got some action that night in the form of David who was studying technical drawing at university and his Dad was a Maths teacher. They had left the disco for a walk and he'd cornered her down an alleyway and turned into a "rampant, panting octopus" apparently. Sark escaped; he was a crap kisser anyway. At the same time, Flee was getting frustrated as she was not making much progress with Jesus, which probably had something to do with his lemon-sucking girlfriend, Marie-Jose, hovering around like a dark cloud. Back when we were in Marilyn's parents' house, Nathan had been severely reprimanded because he'd been messing about Frank Spencer-style as he tried to fold up the bed-settee and got caught inside it with one leg hanging out. The ensuing row took them into the bathroom where Flee could hear everything they were saying. Schmoozy Nathan calmed her down eventually with sweet nothings, culminating in thc priceless one-liner: "Marilyn, later on I am going to make you as taut as a violin string". From that moment we coined Nathan's phrase forever more when in situations like now with a lot of kissing and not much else:

"I feel a bit violin-stringy" Flee said "All this kissing is driving me insane, even if we wanted to do anything there'd be nowhere to do it, they all live in barracks and we can't take them to our stinky car."

The car did stink so we took it for a makeover at the garage. We hoovered, wiped, de-cluttered, even picked wild flowers and put them on the dashboard. After that we went for a bracing walk in the mountain air and I gave them all a singing lesson with my warm-up tape which Philip, my singing teacher, had given me. It blew away the cobwebs and made us a bit giddy so we stuck on a Jacques Brel tape and pranced about doing improvised contemporary dance which we'd seen plenty of and could easily mimic and lampoon. Best bit of exercise we'd had in weeks. Sark's new party trick was pulling off her normally tight jeans without undoing any buttons. She was so thin they just slid off her; she needed to get a belt.

The next day was Valentine's Day. The weather was good so we decided to walk down to the area where I had spent my 'free day' so I could show them the old bridges. We took a slightly different route this time and came upon an interesting and abandoned old building with no roof. In our constant quest for treasure and curios (blame Enid Blyton) we went inside and rummaged around. Flee picked up a lovely piece of old tile and Sark found a photo of a young soldier (how apt!). I stayed inside to see what I could discover and heard the others outside and a Spanish man's voice. I glanced out of the window and there was a skinny gipsy asking them for money so out I sauntered:

"No go away, no money!" I said confidently.

Sark then froze, turned to me and out of the corner of her mouth said:

"He's got a knife,"

He most definitely did have a fuck-off girt knife with a rusty jagged edge and was brandishing it towards Flee's stomach where she had her bum-bag.

"Money! Money!" He demanded.

I didn't actually have my purse on me; I had left it in the car that morning. I was however saying over and over in my head "please don't take my walkman, please don't take my walkman." At this point an older man and his dog walked past slowly along the ridge above us. He was carrying a shotgun and could see what was going on. He just ignored it, maybe he was even in on it so we decided we had to play ball. Sark gave the gipsy the equivalent of thirty quid.

"Money! Money!" He shouted.

He still wasn't satisfied and wanted more. The gipsy got closer to Flee's bag and made her open it. She had a wad of traveller's cheques and she hesitated while trying to explain that it wasn't real money.

"Money! Money!" He was getting angry now

"Give him the cheques Flee and he'll leave us alone, we can claim them back later" I said in a panic.

"Okay, good idea," she said. Her poor little hands were trembling as she got out the cheques.

Finally he left us alone and sloped off casually towards the shanty town by the

Moorish baths. We were in shock and walked back to the car shaking. We went straight to the police station to report the mugging. The policemen were like characters in Accidental Death of an Anarchist by Dario Fo. It was all rather comedic. They got out a book of mug shots and asked us if we recognised our assailant. After the turn of a few pages we all recognised him and pointed directly at the same image. The police all laughed in a 'oh not him again' fashion. They took our statements, made a report, gave us paperwork for the bank and we left. We then had a vaso de leche in Cristina to try and cheer ourselves up with the hope of seeing Jesus and his Disciples. An annoying soldier called Manuel had recently latched himself onto Flee scuppering all chances of her desired union with Jesus. Manuel was a know-all who spoke very good English thus 'trumping' all the other lads who didn't. He demanded her attention and was a 'dope bore' who always talked about ganga and "the biggest joints in the world". Tonight of all nights we wanted to avoid Manuel but he managed to track us down and proceeded to tell us all off and give us a lesson in self-defence. Bit late now, mate! Later in the car we were smoking away as usual (although we now had our Hotel Ibis ashtray) contemplating our day: "Drugs, violence, rock 'n roll but where is the sex?" Flee enquired.

There is a branch of The National Westminster Bank in San Pedro down on the coast and this was the only bank where we could redeem Flee's travellers' cheques. We fired up the Renault 5 and got back on that winding, hairpin-bend-a-plenty road and I bought sweets for the journey. I hated being back on the costa. There was a bad vibe about the place and San Pedro was a 'stuck on town' with horrible plastic fronted 1-storey shop units and generic bars. The bank had a pink frontage and not the usual NatWest black & silver signage; bad omen that pink plastic. We ventured in and Flee spoke to a dinny man behind the counter who was unhelpful. He told her that he could not give her any money without a written letter from the police although she had a report from them. She burst into tears so I marched up to the desk and demanded to see the manager. Half an hour later a bitch in a power suit with dyed-blonde hair appeared:

"You were told by my assistant that you need an official letter," she sneered

"But she has a report" I said.

"I need a letter," She snarled.

"We can't go back to Ronda, we've no petrol and no money!" screamed Flee.

"I cannot help you; I need a written letter from the police in Ronda," said the woman.

"Can't you just phone the police in Ronda and get them to verify it or fax you a letter?" I asked

"No, we cannot do that, you need to go back to Ronda and come back here tomorrow with the letter!" She insisted.

"You're a really unhelpful bitch, aren't you?" I said

We turned on our heels and left the bank; Flee was in floods of tears so we went to a bar and I called NatWest head office and thrashed it out on the phone with them. They were very helpful and told me to take Flee back into the bank in half an hour and it would all be sorted out. Bingo! We triumphantly swished though the double-doors like Charlie's Angels and asked for the manageress who soon appeared with egg all over her face and motioned the cashier to pay Flee her money. We'd won!

We put it all behind us and drove back to Ronda, laughing all the way. Three more days until the Clarkes arrived and we wanted to spend it in our favourite places with our favourite soldiers and hopefully steal a kiss or two. That night we had a pool competition, England v Spain, with Juan, Nicolas, Beardy Binzie and a bloke we called Dense (because he was). England won. We had managed to shake off Manuel by going to some new bars and had garnered enough Spanish to explain to the others that Flee wasn't interested in him and that in fact he was annoying and not to tell him where we were.

On our last night, we were outside the bullring when I saw a familiar face walking up the street. It was none-other than Giuseppe, he was back! I took my leave of the girls and agreed to meet them at 'Cinderella time' beside the trucks at a quarter to eleven. It started to snow heavily and was settling on the town so Giuseppe and I ran down Calle Virgen de la Paz, skidding all the way and laughing before finding a warm bar with sofas where we sat and kissed all evening. Time passed too quickly that night and when we got up to leave and went outside, everything was bright and white and beautiful in the snow. I walked him to Plaza del Socorro where Flee and Sark were bidding farewell to the others. They knew we were leaving the next day so it was hugs-all-round and we stood in the square and waved them all off, snow falling around us, the lot of them shouting, singing and jumping up and down in the truck and blowing kisses. We watched them disappear around the corner, heard their cheers and songs fade into the night then promptly went to the nearest bar and burst into tears. We'd had such a wonderful time with our soldiers and we'd miss them. "That's life on the road, babe!" said Flee.

Chapter Nine
Gibraltar

Leaving Ronda was sad. It was Sark's turn to drive, Flee ate sweets and I shut myself off with my Walkman and some Chopin. We took a different route down this time as we wanted to have a change. It was snowy and woodlandy and pretty but we were all melancholy. After some map shenanigans we located the golf course and the estate where Sark's parents were staying. It was a completely different kind of Spain compared with what we were used to in our beloved Ronda but we had to look on the bright side: finally a decent meal, a bed and a free washing machine courtesy of Sark's family. We crashed out in a luxurious white, turreted villa which was very 'Joe & Ken' and proceeded to cover their kitchen floor in dirty washing. It was nice to be spoilt for once. We had agreed not to tell them anything about the mugging, they'd only worry and nag. They passed on letters to Flee and I from our parents with news from back home. All was well. The first night we ate far too much and all got merry on wine and Sark's Dad was being a pubber and sang rude songs:

Old Ma Nelly
With a bamboo belly
And tits held up with string
Sitting on the grass
With a finger up her arse
Playing God Save The King

Auntie Sharyn shared her fags with us but Sark dipped out because her parents didn't know that she smoked although she's been at it for years. They took us to an Italian restaurant in Duquesa and more merriment ensued. Soon after, however, we realised that they were on holiday and we were ruining their fun so the next morning we finished off our washing, filled our bellies and made our way towards Gibraltar. Uncle Bryan videoed us leaving with his fancy camera thing.

Our map distinctly told us where the Rock was but we couldn't seem to find a signpost telling us where to turn off, just notices for Spanish supermarkets, campsites and other Spanish towns.
"Are you sure we are on the right road?" Said Sark.
"Yeah, it says so on the map," I said. "Pass Guadiaro, Sotogrande then there should be a turning, have we passed a place called San Roque?"
"Yep, just passed that." Said Sark.
"Where is it then, why isn't it sign posted?" Asked Flee.
"Perhaps it's too small to be signposted?" I offered.
The weather was dreadful and we kept on going trying to locate Gibraltar.
"Algeciras coming up!" Cried Sark.
"We've passed it then, Algeciras is way too far, turn around at the next cambio," I said.
As we turned the car Sark let out a gasp.
"There it is, there it is, that's Gibraltar!!!"
Across a small bay was a huge mountain sticking out of the sea, it was an incredible sight.
"I never thought it was that big," said I "thought it was a rock face like Beachy Head but with a few monkeys hanging off it."
"Don't you watch Blue Peter Beck?"
Much like my warped pre-vision of the Louvre, I confessed to knowing nothing about Gibraltar, never having seen any pictures. The only reason I wanted to go there was to say that I'd 'done it', find some work, bump up the coffers and move on to Portugal for the next leg of our journey. I had an innate dread of squaddies and skates and presumed that Gibraltar would be full of them, puking on street corners and picking fights.
We eventually found our way to the Gibraltar frontier which was difficult and the only thing that made it possible was a dirty-great rock leading us the way which you could hardly miss. We pulled up at customs:
"Hello, what is the purpose of your visit?" Asked a bloke with epaulettes.
"We're on holiday," I said all blasé.
"How long are you staying?" He asked sternly.
"One month," I said.
"Where are you staying?" He asked.
"Erm, in an hotel?" I said nervously.
"Okay, move on; don't sleep in your car". He smiled at last.
Was the guy telepathic? How did he know we would sleep in our car? It was the first time we felt uneasy with the authorities, everyone else had just ignored us.

We motored across a runway which was like a railway level-crossing with barriers that went up and down whenever a plane landed, cool.
"Let's drive to the end and look at Africa, you must be able to see it from there!" I begged in anticipation.
We couldn't contain our excitement, it was like being on the edge of a giant map (which it was really but you know what I mean). We followed the lighthouse signs to Europa Point but the roads wound round in intricate one-way systems and suddenly we were driving up a steep narrow street and into the old town.
"This is beautiful, all these buildings are lovely," I said.
"It's a lot like Genoa isn't it?" said Sark.
"Exactly," I said. I remembered that lovely Italian town with fondness.
"Nice shutters," said Flee and again she found herself in roof heaven.
"Never in a million years did I think it was going to look like this, I love it!" I exclaimed.
We managed to double-back and get on the correct road to Europa Point, through some very narrow tunnels and out on the other side where Africa in all its glory was spread out in front of us. We parked our car on the wasteland at Europa Point and walked as near to the edge as we could. There were some telescopes you could pay a few pennies for to see the view but it was so close you didn't need to use them. Everything was clear, like the Isle of Wight from Portsmouth but without the dreaded and nightmare-inducing Spithead forts. The Straits of Gibraltar, gateway to the Mediterranean knocked the Versailles canals off the top spot of my 'best and majestic views' list.
"Oh look, it's my dream house!" I again exclaimed.
"Where?" Asked Flee.
"Down there, over that wall," I pointed.
We all peered over a wall and below were some old white cottages right on the edge of the cliff next to the lighthouse. There was a sign saying 'No Entry' so we were unable to walk down the hill and go up close to the lighthouse and its cottages. What an amazing place to live, right at the end of Europe.
"The last house in Europe," we said.
We went back into town to find a suitable place to park our car for the night but it wasn't easy and there weren't that many opportunities. We really needed to move out of our car but we had to find work first as we were all down to our last fifty quid. It was amazing that we'd got this far on five-hundred, it had been two months now.
We ventured onto Gibraltar's main drag which funnily enough was named 'Main Street' and succumbed to a Wimpy which wasn't that good. We passed lots of English shops but on the whole Gibraltar had a weird and interesting, exotic bazaar (even bizarre) feel about it; a lot of Indians in the shops and Moroccan men

in djellabas standing in doorways. Huge bunches of coriander and mint hung from tiny little kiosk-style establishments and there was a distinctly laid-back feel about the place. We saw people on mopeds, with no helmets, driving around with massive girt joints hanging out of their mouths. This was not at all like the revolting Naval Base we'd assumed. We carried on up past Marks & Spencer and entered a Safeway mini-supermarket but stopped dead in our tracks, mouths aghast in three 'O' shapes. A packet of 20 Silk Cut was 57p. Only 57p! Cheaper than the ferry, cheaper than France and even cheaper than Spain. This was the best news we'd had in days. We spent the evening wandering around town and some oiks asked us if we wanted to go to a place called The Brass House. They looked like squaddies so we ignored them and ducked down a side street into Irish Town and had a coffee in The Ark Royal, a small bar run by a Moroccan bloke who chatted away to us. Later on we realised that the TV in the corner was showing porn, hard core porn but with people dressed in Louis IV wigs shagging on brocade-covered chaise longues. We decided to make a swift exit.

Chapter Ten
Lips Like Figs

The next morning I had an agonising experience. The wet-wipes had become loose from their lid so I poked them back into the plastic hole but did so the wrong way and couldn't get my finger out; the more I pulled the more those tiny triangular pieces of plastic dug in and the more my finger started to go purple. I wedged a knife in to set my finger free – pure agony!
We had slept in our car parked up against the wall of an office block called Regal House but found that there were too many people around. Gibraltar is not a city and it's not a village, somewhere in-between but not good for living in the car. We decided that we should perhaps park at Europa Point instead although Flee read in her book that we could stay in an old barge down at the marina which did lodgings and sounded quite romantic. We walked to a place called Piccadilly where we got washed and ready to go bar-to-bar asking for work. We had read that we didn't need a work permit here like in Spain so it shouldn't be too difficult. After some asking around we soon discovered that in order to work we needed an address – catch 22. We moseyed on down to Marina Bay to see if we could rub-shoulders with some salty sea dogs who would rent us a boat or give us a job and ended up in 'Charlie's Tavern', a titchy little place full of men and a sourpuss barmaid called Sue. As soon as we got comfortable we were approached by a bloke called Dave Watson who was thirty-two, identical to Ian Dury (including the accent) and was a window cleaner from Paddington. He was nice and friendly and we told him how we'd made it to Gibraltar.
"Do you hablar?" asked Dave.
"No, but we speak a bit of French" We replied.
"Oh, you parlez then do you?" Dave asked in his amusing accent.
"Yes, but we do speak English," we groaned.
Within half an hour Dave was reading my palm, talking astrology and that he'd fallen in love with me and started to name our children. He wanted to take me

"up the rock" tomorrow and even got down on one knee and proposed. It was all causing a merry scene and the place was filling up with men who had finished their Saturday morning shifts and were out drinking their earnings. We also met a lad called Rick, who lived on The Barge (so it was true then) and a Londoner called Roy, who said we could live on his boat for nothing - just chip-in for the food, cook and clean up. We accepted and another round of drinks was ordered from Sue. Everyone was so friendly and the atmosphere was terrific, they were the sort of people who flashed their fags around and called us three 'dentists' because we 'pulled them out one at a time'. We had a fabulous afternoon in Charlie's with lots of laughter, jokes and banter and it was refreshing to speak our own language with fellow kin. There was one bloke however who kept his distance and stayed up at the bar shooting over the odd disapproving look in our direction. He stood out not only for that, but for what he was wearing: the tiniest, tightest, cut-off jean-shorts, with bare legs and blue deck shoes. On top he had a blue woolly jumper. He was well over six foot and very slim with blond hair, blue eyes and a dodgy moustache. Roy called over to him.
"Hey Klaus, are you playing tonight?"
Klaus, of course! He was German; he had to be wearing those clothes.
"Yeah, it's a re-match," said Rick
"Ha! I'll thrash the lot of you with one hand! Take you all on!" said Klaus
They were talking about table-tennis and this Klaus was the 'Table King' apparently. They all played on a table which was set up on The Barge and they invited us round for the evening. Outside Charlie's there were two tasty surfer-types with long hair, one blonde and one dark and they had a shaggy black dog with them called Batman who wore a red neckerchief. The blonde one caught my eye and started to wink at me; he was lovely but had a missing tooth but it sort of added to his charm. His name was Pascal and his mate was called Pedro and they were Belgian and lived on an old wooden boat. We stumbled out of Charlie's with Roy and went to get our stuff to take it to his boat. He forgot to mention that his boat wasn't actually moored in the marina but in a little free-mooring called Scott's Yard. I don't know how we managed it but all of us scrambled into a dingy with our bags and rowed over to Hawk, a modern yacht which didn't actually belong to Roy - he was just "looking after it for some French bloke". Roy gave us three the large cabin at the bow (his was in the stern) and told us how to use everything, how to lock-up and not to use too much water if we could help it as to fill up the tank meant sailing over to the quayside marine petrol station. We got sorted and went over to The Barge which was also in Scott's Yard but moored up although it did involve balancing over rickety gangplanks to be able to board. Apparently two people had fallen in and died over the years due to being either sloshed, stoned or a lethal cocktail of both. There were plenty of boats in the yard

of varying shape and size, some moored some on anchor; all sorts of people lived there and not just the hippies and the travellers but also 'normal' people who had full-time jobs and kids. There were cables and lines everywhere, not much lighting, slippery surfaces, bits of wood poking out all over the shop, masts clanking, dogs barking, people in the dark swearing and cursing and skinning up in cars. On entering The Barge (its actual name was Malymot) one was amazed by the sheer interior space, a lounge, a large kitchen, toilets, a shower and a full-size table tennis table set up at the back. It was an old Dutch barge, wooden and painted and the real frigging deal when it came to boating stuff. There was a great big mast in the middle of the room and a proper stove. There were men everywhere, making their dinner, watching TV, reading in a corner and we were soon introduced to the owner, a boy of fifteen called Jerry who looked like Vanilla Ice.

"Oi Jerry, we need some more bog roll, that copy of Papillion is down to its last pages" said Rick.

"Go and buy some then, you're earning," replied Jerry.

"Just telling you that's all," Rick said.

Jerry was at Bayside School, the local comprehensive down the road and he was very hospitable and friendly.

"Cup of tea girls?" Jerry asked.

We got chatting to a bloke called Alan who filled us in a bit. Alan was a Londoner who was our sort of age with a nice, honest face and "hair like a fun wig" as Sark observed.

"Jerry's great, a diamond, amazing how he does it really," said Alan

"Where are his parents?" We asked.

"Dad left, and Pam's in K G Five" said Alan

"Who's Pam?" We asked.

"You don't know Pam? Jerry's Mum innit" Explained Alan.

"What's K G Five?" I asked.

"Local nuthouse. She comes out now and again and sees him but she doesn't talk to anyone, not even Jerry. She tried to set up a log fire in the middle of the barge floor last week because she thought it was cold. She had to be escorted back up there".

In the course of the evening we drank a lot more and Sark got chatted up by Black Danny, the straw-hat-wearing 'shot away' Caribbean, who was mesmerised by her green eyes and wouldn't leave her alone:

"I've been watching you for three weeks, Greenie," said Danny.

"I only got here yesterday," Sark said.

"You gave me your address in Amsterdam, have you forgotten that already?" Danny was right up in her face at this point, "You are lying to me Greenie and you are hurting me."

Alan stepped in and saved Sark from Danny, Flee cosied up with Roy and I ended up in the arms of Pascal, the sexy Belgian surfer. They told us about the history of The Barge and what famous people had visited in the past including Rod Stewart who rocked up one night with a blonde bimbo, pissed, went through their cassette collection and stuck on one of his own Greatest Hits albums until they got fed up and threw him out because he was waking up the babies. A great night was had by all but I don't know how we got back on the Hawk without falling in. We slept very well in the cabin until the sun rose over the Rock the next morning.
"Do you want to come to Ceuta with us today?" Roy asked
"Urghhh. What time is it?" Flee moaned.
Before we had a chance to ready ourselves, the decks of Hawk were awash with men clambering aboard and untying the ropes. Although it was Roy's boat, Klaus was the one who seemed to be in charge and he was giving orders which everyone just followed...Germans. He never even bothered to say hello to us - just started swearing at the others and taking the wheel. Soon after, we set sail towards Africa with Roy, Klaus, a young lad called Richard, Rick, Pedro and Pascal. They each took turns at the wheel apart from Klaus who swiftly unfolded a table and slapped a backgammon board down, "Right, who's up for a gammoning?"
Pascal was all over me like an octopus and I didn't like to canoodle in front of everyone else so I tried to watch the game but was soon feeling queasy and spent the next hour below deck throwing up, which did the trick with the Pascal issue if nothing else. We docked at Ceuta and they all jumped off but I didn't feel like going so I told them all to head off without me and I lay down inside. Five minutes later, Klaus was in the galley stirring into a cup of boiling water with a spoon. He slammed the cup down on the table in front of me.
"Drink this!" Klaus ordered.
"What is it?" I said in a pitiful fashion.
"Hot marmite, go on drink, it'll make you feel better."
I obeyed, you didn't disobey Klaus.
"Good. Now drink this!" And he slammed down a glass of something in front of me.
"What is it?" I asked.
"Southern Comfort, go on drink, it'll make you feel better," Klaus said, his tone slightly softening now.
Again I obeyed and he was right.
"Come on, time for some fresh air. On the way back I am going to let you steer the boat, it'll stop your sea-sickness," he insisted.
"Okay Klaus."
We all spent an hour or so playing pool in a bar and had some tapas. Ceuta is a

Spanish enclave so not really Morocco and the place just seemed like Spain really – at least inside that bar.
Klaus kept to his word and got me to take the wheel for the journey back and I didn't feel sick once. Pascal rekindled his interest and had his hands all over me while I was trying to steer, whispering "sleep with me tonight" in my ear. I had really lost interest in him and shrugged him away. We anchored in the yard and then all went to Charlie's.
"Coffee brandy?" Klaus asked
"Urgh no, I've never had a coffee brandy."
"Never had a coffee brandy?! Sue, give us two coffee brandies please." Sue rolled her eyes and fixed the drinks.
It was a day of firsts and I spent the rest of the evening getting to know Klaus, who was really interesting and funny, even though he was a woolly-hat-wearing, salty old sea dog with a missing front tooth (like most of them). I also learnt a new expression, well two really: tranquilo as in relax, and 'tranqued-out' as in 'let's go back to the boat and just tranq-out'. Rick in particular said it all the time, that's when he wasn't talking about dope or juggling.
Today we enquired about opening a bank account but they wanted £500 minimum. Madness - whatever happened to 'open a bank account with one penny?' We would have to make do with stuffing our money under the mattress, that's when we could manage to actually earn any money. We continued with our job hunting and by the end of the day we had all struck it lucky and found jobs. Flee and Sark got positions as waitresses in Pizza Hut in Casemates and I got a post doing all-sorts at Uncle Tom's Cabin in Cornwall's Parade.
Roy's boat was great but it didn't have a shower so we had to run-the-gauntlet by sneaking into Marina Bay, Sheppard's Marina or Victoria Stadium which wasn't easy. We had already been kicked out of the stadium twice and 'Dennis the Wanker', Pier Master of Marina Bay, was always on the lookout for any 'yardies' trying to use his showers. Our Renault 5 had died a death but we were not really using it anyway and just parked it somewhere safe. Gibraltar is so small you could walk everywhere. Klaus and Roy offered to fix the car as they could put it on the ramp at their workshop. Klaus was the maintenance mechanic for all the machinery and cranes on the huge Europort construction site over on the west side of Gibraltar and Roy also worked there as a labourer.
"French mechanics?" Klaus said shaking his head. "No such things, Spanish neither."
We eagerly agreed to let a German fix our car, it was a given.
We were rapidly getting to know Gibraltar and how things were done around here. We now had an address as such because Roy verified he was our landlord (or even sealord) so we went to register for an ID Card and queued up in a 1970s

office where the civil servants smoked at their counters. An old man who was very short came in and started shouting at everyone in a loud, high-pitched voice and then promptly left. A man pointed at my trainers and said:
“They cost £79”

“No they didn’t, I got them for £29 in the sale actually,” I retorted.
That night we watched the local TV station GBC which showed episodes of Dallas, followed by an incredible program called Telebingo hosted by a be-suited man called, Andy, who was flanked by two dolly-birds who called out bingo numbers. I didn’t really get it until Roy explained that you would buy your bingo cards in the local shops and then tick off the numbers at home. They were all coded and computerised so if you won you’d go up to Broadcasting House and collect your cash prize. Bingo! I liked it.
GBC also had a radio station which was far too ‘middle of the road’ for us but quite informative. The other option was BFBS forces radio absolutely atrocious and even Simon Bates would be cringing, it was ‘so forces’ and would advertise all sorts of exciting-sounding activities, none of which you could go to unless you were in the forces. However it would provide us with entertainment when cleaning with ‘Everybody Dance Now’ and ‘Wiggle It Just A Little Bit’ which Klaus would try and sing along to in his German accent - “Viggle it sust a liddle bid”. We soon discovered a Spanish radio station, Los Cuarenta Principales, which was what you’d expect from a Top 40 station but without the annoying English forces banter.
Today I had my first ever encounter with a cockroach - a horrible business! One of my tasks was to clean the toilets in the bar first thing and on this particular morning, a large brown thing with legs scuttled around full-speed and I had to go and get Salah, the chef, to kill it for me. Later I saw another one lying in the kitchen sink. Cockroaches have now surpassed spiders as my demons of hate. It was blowing a gale today and getting on the dingy was no fun but once inside it was all cosy and Klaus came over to cook.
“Hope you like liver,” said Klaus, all excited.
“Love it!” I said
“Not really,” said Sark, but she was willing to eat it.
Flee is a veggie so liver was off but she actually did try some in the end because she was hungry and it smelled delicious. Klaus lived on a small seven-metre wooden sailing boat called Meerschaum, about 20m away from ours. He had a lodger called Edgar who had a lot of teeth missing and those that remained were all brown. He was also German but couldn’t speak a lot of English, mainly profanities, so conversation with him was limited. Edgar earned good money and was always eating in Bianca’s but always ate the same thing - “Steak-Chips-

Pepper-Sauce" and wouldn't eat anywhere else and would sit on his own. Flee was sporadically getting-off with Roy and a little relationship was starting to blossom. Klaus, Roy, Richard, Sark, Flee and I spent most evenings together on Hawk sharing the cooking, washing up and then playing backgammon or lie-dice. Klaus would always watch the news on the telly and start swearing at it: "Fucking Saddam Hussein!" he'd belt out. The winds would be whistling above and the boat would roll like a pig but it was great fun and we were finally earning money and saving up for the next leg of our adventure. One such night, Richard went home, Sark went to bed and Flee and Roy went to his cabin for a 'massage'. Klaus and I stayed up talking and he told me that he needed to kiss my lips because they looked like "open figs". How can a girl resist a comment like that so I obliged but I wasn't sure about him. He was 30 years old for God's sake and I was 21 and until then we all referred to Klaus as "some old git who's quite good at cooking". I went to my cabin and he went to his boat. In the morning I confessed to the others:

"You never guess what I did last night" I blurted.

"What" They replied

"Don't laugh, will you?" I said.

"Tell us! We won't laugh" Said Sark.

"I... I kissed Klaus" I said gingerly.

"What's wrong with that, he's lovely!" they exclaimed.

It was then I realised that Klaus was indeed 'lovely' and interesting, and kind; he could sail, he could fix things, he could cook, he did his own washing and he had a steady job.

The next day was awkward and I was dreading seeing Klaus. He turned up at the boat that afternoon with Richard and we were all sitting out on deck.

"Right you lazy bitches, get in the dingy, time for some work!" Klaus boomed.

The other two sat there and refused to budge but I obediently got in the dingy with them and they took me to the slipway and handed me a spatula.

"Scrape all the barnacles off the bottom of this boat," Klaus ordered.

I did as I was told and afterwards we went back to the boat to eat and play backgammon. Klaus was in a mood which grew worse as I kept getting lucky with my doubles and beat him three times in a row. He soon left under a cloud to go to the showers with Roy. Roy returned without Klaus:

"He's gone home Beck, got the right hump," said Roy.

"He's not coming over then?" I asked, dejected.

"Don't think so. If you want to see him get in the dingy and go over there, Edgar's not around tonight," replied Roy.

"It's raining and windy," I moaned.

Roy just shrugged.

Right, I'm going to brave it! I got in that dingy and made my way over, it wasn't easy, the wind kept blowing me back to Hawk and the dingy was filling up with rain. As I neared Meershaum, I shoved my hands under the icy water and grappled around to try and find a rope to cling on to but they were all slimy and the dingy was starting to tip over. Eventually I managed to haul myself towards the hull and I could see an orange glow through the portholes. It all looked rather cosy in there but would he let me in? I tapped on one of the little round windows.
"What!" Klaus's voice bellowed from inside.
"Klaus it's me, can I come in?" I squeaked.
"Make sure you tie up that dingy properly!" He said moodily.
I clambered aboard and Klaus was lying on his huge triangular bed at the bow of the boat reading a Herman Hesse novel. I sat on Edgar's bunk which was the only place to sit and perused my surroundings. Everything was so neat and tidy and properly stowed-away to prevent accidents when the boat rocked. He had a little kettle on a perfectly shiny gas stove and a black & white TV on a shelf above the counter held in place with octopus straps. The only down-side was the toilet. When I asked where it was he said "Outside; bucket & chuck it". Oh how unromantic!
"Want a cup of tea?" Klaus asked
"Alright," I said merrily.
"Can you make me one too, I'm knackered."
He seemed very gruff but soon warmed up. He told me where all the things were and I noticed that he had everything in little pots and also used brown sugar instead of white. Klaus's boat was a revelation and so was he. The other thing I noticed was his body. All this time he had covered it up with layers of shrunken wool but here he was, sitting up in his bed in all his post-showered opulence bearing his strong muscular arms and chest. I could give you the excuse that I never went back to Hawk that night because of the weather but I'd be lying.

Chapter Eleven
"I'm Totally Sorry Mate"

Flee and I now had lovers but Sark was yet to find one although she wasn't short of offers in the form of Black Danny, George, the Czechoslovakian, who gave her a red rose, Richard, who had a nice body but was "far too young", and Alan from The Barge who asked her to go to the pictures and watch Home Alone. She politely refused them all but spent time with Alan as she liked him "as a friend" and he was a fellow artist and amateur photographer. Klaus told me that he might have a job in Malta and went out to see someone about it; I was spending every night on his boat now and we were becoming very close. I didn't want him to go to Malta but couldn't really say anything because we were just 'passing through' ourselves, it was all emotionally confusing as we got on so well; that night he taught me how to foxtrot and we danced away on Hawk to Dizzy Gillespie and then he broke into a jolly German song about Pigalle in Paris which he often sung whenever we spoke about France: "Pigalle, Pigalle Das ist die große Mausefalle mitten in Paris!". Klaus amused us all with 'hairy stories of the sea' and tales of his German childhood in the Black Forest, and multiple motorbike and car accidents he'd been involved in. He was adopted at the age of nine months, his birth-mother was a "nice girl from a nice family" who got pregnant by the "town rogue" and her Father forced her to give her baby up for adoption. Klaus lay in an orphanage until his adoptive-Mum and her friend came and picked him out of dozens of screaming babes who needed homes. He was lying there "smiling and beautiful" and it was his Mum's friend who actually chose him. It was a charming account of something rather sad and emotional. I had never met anyone who had been adopted.

There was a job going in the kitchens of Pizza Hut so I handed my notice in at Uncle Tom's and moved to 'The Hut' - better surroundings, more hours and working with Sark and Flee was going to be fun. I was going to miss Salah, though, because I enjoyed working in the kitchen with him. He was always humming his own 'mix' of tunes usually Bolero followed by Yesterday and La Cucaracha. I made an appointment to see a doctor at the health centre so I could go on the pill and after a 4-hour wait I was attended to and when I requested 'the pill' he asked "are you married?" I grimaced and there was a 'pregnant' pause; he scribbled out the prescription and I left.

Sunday 10th March was Flee's birthday and she was turning 22. We bought her a salty-sea-dog woolly hat, a pair of funky psychedelic leggings and 200 Fortuna Light cigarettes. That evening we had a party on Hawk and everyone came. Sark fell in the water coming back from work. This had happened to me the previous week when I lost my footing on the slipway and slid down slow-motion on the slimy green stuff and plop! Into the cold, dirty water.

It was all getting intense with Klaus. He told me he had turned down the Malta job because he couldn't leave me, he had fallen in love and he didn't know what to do. "It's like getting a double-six in backgammon and not being able to move," he said. Things were ticking over nicely with us girls and we were saving money and talking about the next step, Flee wasn't attached to Roy at all, he was "just good in bed" and would "do for the meantime". We went out sailing when we could, brought home cold pizza to the boat and had regular parties with the yard crowd. Some Saturdays we would walk over to Spain and party in La Linea. That was one wild town; people skinning-up on the bar at Casablanca, snorting speed off the toilet cisterns in The Fox. The town was really run-down but at night it all 'lit up'. By now we were getting to know a few people, some other girls from work or in the marina bars, and we couldn't walk past Charlie's without being called in for a drink. Old Charlie, the owner, let us use the bar as an address and we had letters from home sent there and he and Klaus were mates and would drink together and talk about growing turnips.

Wednesday 20th March 1990 was my 22nd birthday. Klaus went to work and we three girls all happened to have the day off so treated ourselves to lunch at the posh Danish restaurant, The Little Mermaid, and I received some lovely presents: a Moroccan blanket, a t-shirt, The Complete Plays of Oscar Wilde and some Body Shop creams and a romantic evening in with Klaus.

By coincidence, a guy we knew from Havant was living on The Barge. His name was John but he was never one of our good mates so we decided not to bother meeting up with him, just said our hellos and left it at that. Sark went up to see the apes with Czechoslovakian George who was looking for a "tall slim wife" and had obviously found what he was looking for in Sark but sadly she did not feel the same. He later got drunk and appeared on Hawk, wearing a new suit and brandishing a bottle of whisky.

A few days passed and, in the words of Billy Liar, "today was a day for big decisions". I managed to get Flee and Sark on their own and asked them for advice.

"I really love Klaus but I don't want to stay here right now, I want to carry on with you two to Portugal"
"Okay, just come back afterwards," Said Flee.
"I don't want to leave it hanging like that, he'll be heart-broken when we go and worry all the time," I replied.
"And?" Asked Flee.
"I was thinking of asking him to marry me," I said tentatively.
"Ask him then," they casually suggested.
"What, you don't think I'm being a bit rash?" I exclaimed.
"Go on, it'll be good for a laugh!" (An often-used turn of phrase)
And so I did. That evening I sat Klaus down on Meerschaum and popped the question:
"Klaus, will you marry me?" (I was stirring a cup of tea at the time)
"Are you sure?" Klaus said.
"Yes, I have thought this all through, I love you and you love me and you want to take the boat out of the water and do it all up and I would only get in the way so I thought you could do all that while we carry on the rest of our trip and when I come back hopefully Edgar would have moved out and we can live on here together and....."
"Yes, I'll marry you!" He gleefully butted in.
"When?" I asked.
"As soon as possible!" He cheered.
Suddenly we had a wedding to plan on a budget. We'd agreed to keep it quiet but Klaus told everyone the next day then got drunk and fell asleep on Hawk.
Gibraltar is one of those places where you can marry at 24hrs notice - like John Lennon & Yoko Ono did. We went to the registry office and set a date for 12th April 1991 at midday. We had to get a special license (£79), birth certificates sent from home, stuff signed by a lawyer. My Mum was shocked but went along with it and my Dad tried to put me off and told me to wait a bit but nobody else seemed surprised.
It was Good Friday and everything was closed. Flee spent her day off with Roy, and Klaus went over to the yard to 'see a man about a dog' so Sark and I sat on the barge waiting for him. We sat in the lounge area in front of the telly with Old Hippy Pete watching Jesus of Nazareth. Pete nodded to us when we sat down, he was a quiet soul. A man's face on the TV was looking perplexed and sceptical and "Doubting Thomas" Pete piped up in his slow, drawn-out manner. Pam appeared as if from nowhere and sat next to us. "Are you the girl who is getting married?" she asked. "Yes" I said (very long pause). "Oh I do love a wedding" Pam said before getting up and floating away (another long pause). "That's the first time she's spoken to anyone in months" Pete said.

Sark and I noticed that Papillon had finished and they were now onto a copy of The Shining in their loo. Flee spent Good Friday in La Linea with Roy and saw a religious procession where they wore 'Klu Klux Klan' pointy hats and looked rather menacing.

We had not driven the Renault 5 for ages and it sat there in the Marina Bay car park looking all forlorn and sorry for itself. We needed to give it some attention; after all it was going to be my wedding car. Who would have thought the old Renault would be elevated to such a purpose? After some nagging Klaus and Roy fixed the car. I took myself down to Main Street and stopped at the first jeweller's I came across, Montecristo, and bought Klaus a wedding ring, later giving him my ring size. I decided I'd wear red and asked Mum to send out an elegant silk skirt I had, and matched it up with a top from Benetton and some shoes from Torino. Klaus booked us a short honeymoon at a travel-agent in the ICC, 2 nights in the Andalucia Plaza up the coast. We couldn't afford a suit for Klaus so decided to buy one at Marks & Sparks, wear it for the day, air it in the hotel and then take it back (worth a try!). Roy lent him a shirt, tie and shoes and I went to the florist and ordered a bouquet of red roses. We booked a table for lunch at The Viceroy of India and asked Old Charlie if we could have our reception in the bar. He was delighted to oblige. Cards and presents started to arrive and I received two telegrams - one from Sark's parent and another from a mystery sender in Louisville, Kentucky, that simply read 'It should have been me'. To this day, I have wondered who that was...

Friday 12th April 1990 – My wedding day.

Unbeknownst to me, it turned out that Edgar was sharing a flat with four Danish blokes on top of the shop at Europa Point but had preferred to live on the boat with Klaus. Edgar kindly allowed Sark, Flee and I to use his place to have showers and get ready. I had my hen night on Meerschaum the night before and Flee & Sark slept there with me. Klaus did likewise on Hawk with Roy. After all these years as such close friends we could not believe that one of us was actually getting married. Sark and Flee kept saying "you are actually getting married tomorrow Beck" and we'd take another sip of lager. They had both bought a new t-shirt each and they were going to be my purple bridesmaids. They had considered coming dressed as fruit; an orange and a banana, but later (thankfully) shelved the idea. The whole thing was just madness and fun and love - all the ingredients you need for a decent wedding, I suppose. We finally managed to fall asleep although we kept on chatting in the dark much like we used to as 10-year-olds, back in Emsworth, although this time there were no calls from our Mums telling us to be quiet.

We rowed to shore first thing in the morning and picked up my clothes from Sue who had kindly ironed and prepared them beautifully. She gave us all a brandy and then we drove to Europa Point to prepare ourselves. Klaus had never seen me in a dress or remotely dolled up, so I wasn't sure what he would think - mind you, I'd never seen him wear smart clothes either. We had another brandy in the weird little gift shop-come-cafe at Europa Point while we waited for our taxi and headed for the registry office. Klaus was there waiting, all handsome and debonair. He didn't know I was wearing all red so he was surprised but happy. Roy, Rich and George had all turned up in their Sunday best and Edgar wore jeans and trainers. We all moved into the Wedding Room and were greeted by a skinny cadaver of a man who was theatrical and camp but in a Gothic sort of way. He introduced himself as 'Richard John Garcia', heavily rolling the 'R' in Richard. This guy loved to roll his 'Rs' and even if the vows weren't in 'Olde English' he would have said them thus. Klaus was so nervous he couldn't pronounce the words properly and was having trouble with his 'thous' and 'thuses' and everyone was trying not to laugh but couldn't help it. Roy was nearly hyperventilating next to Klaus and the more 'Richard John Garcia' spoke the more everyone laughed. I could sense everyone's shoulders jiggling up and down behind me and I was even having trouble holding it together myself. Then 'Richard John Garcia' spoke up and told them all off.

"I am going to have to stop this ceremony because some people in here are not taking things seriously" he glared around the room. "The Bride and the Groom are behaving impeccably and you are all spoiling the occasion for them". (More laughing due to his glares and his rolled 'Rs'). "I will now leave this room for a few moments in order that you all calm down. And at that, he walked towards the door, turned and added "I will be back shortly to recommence and hope that you are all suitably composed by that time".

All I could hear was Roy saying "I'm totally sorry mate, totally, totally sorry mate" to 'Richard John Garcia' who soon returned and finished off the ceremony. Klaus was so nervous and kept kissing me before it was over and when we exchanged rings and it was concluded 'Richard John Garcia' said "And now the Bride, who has already been liberally kissed, may now be kissed!"

Klaus and I were now married and we left the Registry Office and were pelted with rice and confetti by some of his Danish workmates who had turned up. They then took us all to the Copacabana and bought two bottles of real champagne and our little wedding troupe then walked down Main Street to the Viceroy for a long, boozy lunch which Roy kindly paid for and then gave a speech. Edgar kept moaning and wanted to know why we couldn't have gone to Bianca's and have "Steak-Chips-Pepper-Sauce". Klaus also confessed that he'd got my ring engraved with today's date but the engraver had got it wrong and we could go and change it. I just left it as another symbol of this crazy and momentous day. Klaus and I went our separate ways as agreed, he to The Barge for a kip and a few

games of table tennis and we three went back to Europa Point and played darts, sunbathed and listened to Sticky Fingers by The Rolling Stones. Edgar drove us down to Charlie's later but his car ran out of petrol so I got out and hitched and the first car stopped. The driver took us to a petrol station AND brought us back again - all he wanted was "a kiss from the bride" so I gave him one and he went off waving.
I arrived at Charlie's and a crowd had gathered. Everyone from the yard was there; Annie and her two little girls Lily and Laura, Black Danny, Pascal and Pedro, Jerry plus people from Klaus's work and the bars in the marina. Alan was our 'official photographer', Sue had bought a cake, (some other woman had also made a cake for us), the bar was decorated in balloons and streamers and Old Charlie had got some plastic tables and chairs and arranged them out the front. The party got into full swing and we were given a lot of gifts, 'John Wooden Boat' and his German wife Anna, who lived way out on anchorage, (on a wooden boat) came along with their baby and presented Klaus and I with a beautiful tiny little embroidered white shirt:
"It's for the baby," Said Anna
"What baby?" I said
"Wel,l yours of course, it's why you are getting married so quickly isn't it?"
"She's not pregnant Anna," Klaus laughed.
"Why on earth are you getting married then?"
We all partied for a few hours until Klaus and I left. The whole mob followed us to the Renault 5 which was in the car park covered in 'Just Married' signs; spray foam, balloons and tin cans tied to the back. Everyone was legless at this point although Klaus and I were sober (ish) and Sark was in the arms of Pascal - he never missed a trick that one! I threw my bouquet and a little girl called Sybil caught it, all the other women ran away screaming. We jumped into the car, Klaus honked the horn and they all sprayed the car with beer and we drove off towards the border and on to our honeymoon. We soon got another rather smelly surprise and found that Roy had put a fish under the bonnet, but that didn't mar two days of glorious hotel luxury, drinking Baileys in the bath.

Chapter Twelve
Back On The Road Baby!

We all put in as many hours as possible at Pizza Hut where they all called me 'Alan' because Bruce said I sounded like the TV journalist & presenter, Alan Whicker. Even the managers called me 'Alan'. It was a fun place to work and you got free food but it was chaotically managed by people with no experience. John was particularly irritating and thought he was the 'kipper's knickers' (as Flee's Mum would say). He was only a few years older than us but kept going on about how he used to be a "P.E. instructor in the Army". Then there was nut-job, Julian, haughty Nicky, 'nice' Helen and freak show Denise who would shout her trade-mark 'Hot Food Ladies' and cop at an instant and then have a meltdown in the kitchen screaming, "I am twenty-one and have no social life!" at the top of her lungs in a Canadian accent. It was starting to get really hot now and we'd been sunbathing on the boat when we got the chance which also meant that strange men in cars thought they could call out of their windows to any passing girls:
Grotty Bloke: How's about coming for a spin with us then girls?
Sark: How's about losing some weight first?
Strange how different men of differing nationalities approach strange women. English style is shout out or wolf-whistle, Moroccans just stare, French men say 'Ooh La La' and the Spaniards make a 'soos' sound where they purse their lips and audibly suck in air, or they just slowly shake their heads from side to side, sometimes doing the 'soosing' at the same time.
Roy, Sark, Flee, Klaus and I decided to sail Hawk to Tangier for a short holiday before we had to leave on 7th May. What should have been a six hour journey turned into twelve hours because there was a westerly wind but we were accompanied by leaping dolphins and a star-filled sky. I may not have found my sea legs 100% but I now travelled prepared and took loads of warm clothes to put on as I knew I would be out on deck most of the time. It was a long, slow haul where we kept the boat as near to the Moroccan coast line but not dangerously near

as we had to avoid reefs. Flee cooked us up a bean-feast and we pulled into the port of Tangier just as the sun was rising to the sound of the call to prayer. We moored the boat and sorted out customs. The officials had French-style uniforms and it was all very Casablanca and properly foreign. Klaus made us all jump by suddenly appearing on deck in his underpants and diving overboard into the sea and then who should pop his head out from the hatch of the boat next door but Black Danny, "Hello!" (Yes and he was still wearing that straw hat.)

Tangier was all that I expected and more; I loved it. I was fortunate to have Klaus as my guide because he knew it pretty well and took me on his own tour around to cafes that he'd been to before and speaking to familiar faces all of which were men. There are men everywhere and no women, all the bars are full of men of all ages either playing ludo on wooden boards or watching telly and puffing away on kif pipes. The unnerving thing is that all the men, everywhere, just stare at you. They don't say anything, they don't make any noises or gestures, they just all stare into your eyes.

The walk up to the Grand Socco from the port has you dodging little blue taxis and great big old cream Mercedes which are also taxis. Traffic lights seem to be ignored and forget about zebra crossings! The shops are little cubby-holes which sell spices and cinnamon sticks, henna, brown thick soapy stuff and coffee. Berber women with huge straw hats sit on the side of the road beside baskets loaded with carrots and other vegetables, teapots and cous-cous pans hang from hooks and there is a pungent smell of spice, mint, orange-flower-water and chicken shit all rolled into one. Klaus and I walked through the fish market which was buzzing and noisy, then through slippery alleys to the covered market with butchers' stalls; goats' heads stripped of their skin and eyes, just hanging there all bloody. There were olive sellers with bowls of different types piled up into pyramids, we tried some lemon flavoured ones and some delectable pink ones. The stall holders were quite happy to let us try all the varieties. We ventured under the arches and into the Kasbah; a proper, bazaar feel here and I expected Sidney Greenstreet to be sitting in one of the bars, wearing a Fez. Rows of colourful kaftans and leather slippers, gold plates, painted tables, carpets, pottery, all fabulous and very cheap and I had an urge to buy a house so I could deck it out with all this stuff. We had chicken cous-cous for lunch, bought a few small bits and walked back to the port to find out what the others had been up to. Flee and Sark had not enjoyed their experience as much as I had. Roy had given them the impression that he knew where he was going in Tangier but he didn't and they had been accosted by small urchins who dragged them into a carpet shop and plied them with mint tea and made them feel very uncomfortable.

In the afternoon we all met up and got latched onto by a Moroccan bloke who looked like Roland Gift. He wouldn't leave us alone and Klaus was trying to shake him off but in the end just told him to "FUCK OFF" and they both started arguing and Roland told Klaus he would "cut off his balls". An hour later we were all sitting in Roland's house smoking kif and he told us that he'd met The Rolling Stones and 'Mike' Jagger had been round his house: "Yes, right here in this room, Mike Jagger". His toilet was a hall-of-famer; just a hole in the ground behind a curtain in the kitchen which had a stone placed over it. You would simply boot off the stone, do your business and kick the stone back over the hole, Voila!. Roland's wife was at her sister's house preparing food for a big party because someone had just had a baby. He told us about his brother's chicken who had killed a dog and showed us photographs of the last lamb he and his brother had slaughtered. Roy bought some 'pollen' from Roland so was now very content with the whole Tangier trip.

The sail back to Gibraltar was much quicker with the wind pushing us forward and we could actually get all the sails up and not use the motor. The dolphins appeared again and we were soon safely home. It was a relief to get back to my own boat and be alone with Klaus - there was not a lot of time left now. Klaus cut mine and Sark's hair; this was among the many things he learnt in German National Service along with First Aid, how to drive a truck and how to fix an engine. Flee, Sark and I started to say our goodbyes two days in advance; Alan invited us to his cabin in The Barge and showed us his paintings which were really interesting and I was impressed. We said our goodbyes to the families that lived at that end of the yard, picked up our last pay packets from work and had a little leaving-do, before stocking up on Marmite and peanut butter in Safeway. Klaus had gone to work in the morning but we drove round to the site and had another farewell with him, Roy and the other workmates. Off we sped, leaving a cloud of dust behind us and waving out of the windows, the car fully functional (we hoped). Sark's parting gem was: "Of all the bars in all the world, we had to walk into Charlie's".

We finally left Gibraltar at midday. The plan was to get to Portugal before nightfall but we didn't want to use the Huelva route because it involved getting on a ferry and crossing a river so we drove up via Seville and put our foot down. It was a long old drive and we listened to Los Cuarenta Principales and that dreadfully catchy 'Los Numeros' by Jovanotti kept playing, that along with 'Cuidado con Paloma' had to be the worst two songs in the top forty (apart from Roxette and anything by Michael Bolton). Orange groves and lush green fields abundant, we had the shock of our lives when we saw a giant black bull on a hill in the distance. It was so flipping big with massive horns and we were glad to be in the car. As we got closer and closer the thing just stood there and we realised it was a billboard and not real at all. We kept seeing them after that and laughing at ourselves. We also saw a lot of those roadworks signs that look like my Dad ("Alright Dave!")

We crossed the Spain-Portugal border at Rosal de la Fronterra at 9.30pm and finally stopped for the night at Beja, a town with a striking castle on top of a hill which can be seen from afar and consists of battlemented walls with four square corner towers and a keep. Our guidebook said that you could walk up the 197 steps to the top but we decided to enjoy the view from afar instead. We found a suitable bar which was surprisingly full of women, for a change, and got out the trusty phrasebook and ordered our first Portuguese coffee. I called Charlie's; Klaus and I made an arrangement that I would call Charlie's every Thursday night at 9pm where he would be waiting to receive my call. He was surprised that we had got that far in one afternoon; it was an odd call, didn't seem that we had really parted yet.

Living in a Renault 5 is so much better in the sun, life is so much better in the sun and we made our way to the Portuguese coast and parked up on the beach near Setubal and made a cup of tea. Wow, the Atlantic coast is so different from the Med; vast beaches with white sands that stretch for miles, the feeling of privacy combined with openness and the simple low-rise structures as opposed to rows and rows of hotels and apartment blocks. We sat relaxing, watching two German men in tiny swimming trunks prancing around playing beach-tennis and laughed at their campness. When we tried to leave, our car got stuck in the sand and we had to ask them to help us push it out; pride comes before a fall. The language here is far easier to read than speak even if we did have a phrasebook, it's very guttural and hard to pronounce and you feel as if you are doing an impression all the time. One thing about the Portuguese is that they know how to do toilets; they all had bidets inside the toilets so washing was a dream, we could even wash our feet.

Lisbon was a fantastic capital city: tiled facades, trams, the sea, it had it all, even a weird iron tower which was wedged between two buildings and designed by Eiffel. The Elevador de Santa Justa is actually a lift which connects the lower streets of the Baixa with the higher Largo do Carmo. Lisbon is a very steep capital which leads down to its port and there are a lot of urban lifts, escalators and funiculars in the city but Santa Justa is the only remaining vertical one. This tower is much like La Tour Eiffel in Paris in its metallic simplicity but far smaller and top-heavy. We were all up there with a crowd of other tourists and you got the feeling the thing was going to keel over and we'd all fall out onto the streets screaming. The Luís de Camões Square in the centre was simply breathtaking as far as architecture and tiling was concerned. The walls of the buildings looked like dripping candle wax and were so detailed and white. Even though there were these large open squares the city felt like a miniature model it was so perfect. We'd read about the parish of Belém in our guidebook so made our way there. It is famous

as the place where Portuguese explorers like Vasco da Gama set off on their voyages of discovery and Mrs Ritchie from Emsworth Middle School would have been proud of us for taking the time to go and visit such an historic place. Again we were awestruck by even more amazing architecture with the Torre de Belém and the Jerónimos Monastery but the momentous discovery on our part was the old cake shop Pastéis de Belém founded in 1837. From the outside it seemed like a medium-sized patisserie and café but it had cavernous rooms, covered in blue-and-white tiling, and corridors leading to yet more blue-tiled rooms where waiters walked around carrying huge trays of custard tarts. We went in and ordered tea and tarts and were served these hot little wonders with sachets of cinnamon and icing sugar to sprinkle on top. The place was packed and there were queues at the counter where you could buy the cakes to take away which would be stacked and presented in dainty hexagonal boxes decorated in the blue-and-white patterned theme. That afternoon was spent lazing in the gardens of Belém beside a fountain, dreaming about eating rows of cakes. I finally 'got' what Flee and Sark meant about the simplicity of a custard tart.
Next stop was the town of Sintra, nestled beneath the Sintra Mountains, just north-west of Lisbon, another quaint place with Rapunzel towers, estates, castles and buildings from the 8th and 9th centuries. We stopped off for a wander around the cobbled streets and lapped up the mediaeval experience, caved-in to even more cakes and tea which the Portuguese know how to make properly; you get it in a pot with a separate jug of cold milk.

Pam and Brian, Flee's parents, were on holiday in a village north of Porto called Ofir and were staying in an hotel so we couldn't sleep there but we could use the pool apparently and would be treated to meals. So we headed north to find them and did 300 miles in one day; cassette player on the go full blast, windows open and glorious weather. We passed what can only be described as a makeshift alfresco brothel along the way; three scantily-clad buxom women stood beside a copse on the side of the road, cars with men in them stopped and there were lots of other empty cars parked nearby in what was otherwise barren countryside. Our one cultural stop on the way was the university city of Coimbra, indeed the oldest university in Europe and I could easily understand why it was a seat of learning because the place was full of beauty and history but was also calm, tranquil and organised.
We managed to locate Flee's parents' hotel in Ofir and parked the Renault 5 outside and slept. The next morning, without warning, we surprised Pam and Brian poolside and spent that day with them by the pool, drinking beer and catching up on all the Emsworth gossip. Flee is reading To The Lighthouse by Virginia Woolf and I am reading Narziß und Goldmund by Herman Hesse, recommen-

ded by Klaus (missing him) and there are Germans everywhere. One particular favourite of ours was a fat, bearded one who dived dramatically off the board into the hotel pool shouting 'Geronimo!'

We wandered around the village and loved all the Portuguese pottery but couldn't buy anything obviously. Sark got some film developed and we had a right old laugh at the photos. There was one of us that we'd taken of ourselves in the Ronda bullring in which Sark looked like Steve Miller and Flee looked like "The Puke Bloke from Slade", not Noddy Holder, the other one with the long straight hair. Pam and Brian treated us to dinner that night; we sat outside in the warm evening sun, around a table under a large tree and ate divine grilled octopus and salads, drank good Portuguese wine and a hearty glass of authentic Port to finish off the meal. We promised Pam that we would not have the audacity to park the Renault in their hotel car park so moved it 100 metres up the street instead. Later when we were settling down a man appeared from a nearby bar and put three cans of lager on the bonnet and walked away, cheers mate! We were about to go to sleep but instead we cracked them open, lit up a fag and had a game of cards. Five minutes later three more cans appeared on the bonnet. We agreed that we would spend only two days with Pam & Brian and then head off up to Braga. We didn't want to abuse their hospitality but we were enjoying the grub and also sneaking into their hotel room to shower. Another day was spent poolside and another boozy evening meal ensued and we said our goodbyes after lunch and headed north.

We had a peaceful sleep in a lovely cobbled square and awoke to see a lady with a massive basket of flowers on her head. After days of being spoiled and lounging beside a pool we soon got back into the swing of things as travellers and went to a photography exhibition in Braga entitled 'Grotesque'. There were pictures of animal skeletons and animal parts arranged in montages of a vile nature; 'Pig Snouts' was my particular favourite, although at first I thought they were arseholes.

Portugal was indeed a delightful country despite this bizarre little exhibition; the Belle Époque bars in the cities were unchanged with their old decor and monstrously high ceilings, time stood still in these places but in a good way; the service was excellent and the people friendly but we had to kiss Portugal goodbye and head back into Spain and our travel insurance only lasted until the end of August and we needed to 'pack it in'. We had one of those dismal 'tarmacadam and lorries' drives ("Alright Dave!") which lasted forever until we stopped at Valladolid for the night.

We woke up the next morning behind an old Cathedral which looked very spooky in the dead of night but quite lovely in the morning. Flee told us of her dream where we were in a show with Bruce Forsythe and performed a song

which sounded a bit like Mercedes Benz by Janis Joplin and Stand By Your Man by Tammy Wynette but had different lyrics which she vividly remembered verbatim. We managed to get a tune out of her which wasn't easy because she is tone-deaf and we kept on singing it the whole day.
Oh Lord! Sometimes it's hard to be a lady
Giving all your love to just one man
Oh Lord! Sometimes it's hard to be a lady
But I'm doin' the best that I can!

Valladolid was a great town slap-bang in the middle of the wine-growing region and we spent the day there wandering around the shops, ogling at unusual shoes. We visited the Cathedral and enjoyed yet more opulent Spanish architecture and one particular cavernous bar in the Plaza Mayor had interesting art-deco chairs and tables which I sketched into my diary. The cakes in the shops looked much better than anywhere else in Spain so we bought some and ate them in the Plaza Mayor and witnessed a cycle race which must have been an important one because the whole town was out and there were television crews and cameramen everywhere.

"Who can resist hundreds of fit men in lycra?" Flee smirked

"Gorgeous legs," I agreed.

Thoroughly satisfied with our day in Valladolid, we decided to give ourselves a treat and sampled the local wine, Ribera del Duero - the best I had tasted so far, better than the French stuff even. We drove to El Burgo de Osma and parked in a little plaza outside the church. The priest came out and started speaking to us in Spanish and we wondered what he was saying. He simply wanted to show us his church so we went inside and had a tour. Everyone was very friendly in this small town, an old lady in a shop told us how beautiful we all were, shame we only seemed to get attention from old women and priests, people our own age just ignored us.

It was Thursday so I needed to find a suitable bar with a telephone and the only thing on offer was an 'old man bar' full of topless calendars. Flee called Paul, they kept in touch by letter when we were living in Gibraltar and he said he might be coming to the South of France in June and perhaps he could meet up with us. It seemed he wanted to re-kindle things with Flee but she was a bit wary of him because he kept chopping and changing whilst going out with other women. Flee played it by ear as she was enjoying the single life; it was healthy for her to feel independent. I spoke to Klaus who was in high spirits; he, Roy, Richard and Pascal had "lifted Lobo" and were exhausted but exhilarated. Lobo was a sunken boat that was at the bottom of the sea between Hawk and Meerschaum with its masts poking out. It wasn't that old; it was getting in the way and could be salvaged and sold. The whole operation involved pumps, diving down with big knives and a whole lot of heave-hoing. Klaus told me that Edgar had met a woman and was now living with her and that Richard had moved in to keep him company which was a good idea.

"Oh another thing Rebecca, almost forgot," Said Klaus.

"Yes?" I asked.

"Roy and I found a bolt in the workshop which we think is from one of your wheels."

"What?" I shouted.

"Just go to a garage and ask them to put another one on for you, but do it quickly," Klaus added guiltily.

"Heavens to murgatroyd!" Sark yelled when I told her.

We checked the four wheels and noticed that one bolt was indeed missing. We needed to sort that out pronto and Soria was the next town which hopefully had a Renault garage. The next morning we had to get up early and sort this bolt out so we agreed that whoever woke up first had to sing the first line of the Country song in Flee's dream. It was me and it was funny and we continued to use this method as an alarm clock whenever we needed to get up for something important.

We took the car to a Renault garage and got the bolt fitted, changed money and left Soria. We drove all day, happy with the new bolt, and reached our old haunt Lleida in the evening. We parked up in the exact same spot by the river where we had a few months earlier on 24th January. The atmosphere now was totally different, it was the 'festival of snails' and everyone was wearing snail t-shirts. Snail posters abounded, tents lined the river and inside each tent small parties were going on and each group had a different coloured costume. There was a woman outside stirring two massive pots full of snails in a sauce and some other people doing mad dancing and really getting into it. Live bands with big bass drums were marching through the dust and skipping as they passed. We got into the swing of things ourselves and got sprayed by some kids with water pistols. Lleida brought fruits that hadn't blossomed in the cold winds of winter and it was a bloody good night. We rounded off the bonhomie by listening to The Doors and being surprised by our Benny Hill song coming on at the end and wondered whatever had become of Denim Luc?

The next morning Sark and Flee just had to order a thick chocolate in Lleida for old times' sake as we sat in a bar getting ready to hit Barcelona. "I wish Michael Bolton would cut his bloody hair, he'd look a lot better," Sark said whilst watching MTV.

Chapter Thirteen
Pablo, Antoni, Salvador & Lydia

Today we finally washed, had not done so since the hotel in Portugal. We couldn't arrive in Barcelona unwashed could we? The city we were all dying to see was finally upon us. The traffic was murder but we got into the city centre and put the car in an underground car park and found the Tourist Information in order to get a map. We meandered down Las Ramblas and saw plenty of street theatre and birds in little cages and there was a long-head playing a guitar, accompanied by a woman on a keyboard, just hitting one note monotonously, much like Sparks but totally tuneless. There was a clutch of other long-heads sitting on the ground in front of them swaying from side to side in a trance-like stupor. We visited the Cathedral in the Barri Gothic which had charming plump white geese running around its cloister and then followed the signs to the Picasso museum. Unfortunately it was 400 pesetas to get in so we had a conference and decided that it was far too dear and we would all chip-in for one ticket only. Sark was the lucky winner so she was sent in and told to take her time and come back and describe what she saw - and try and pick up any freebie cards along the way. Flee and I waited outside and wrote in our diaries. Sark emerged later invigorated by Pablo, and armed with cards. The good thing about Barcelona is that you can get your cultural fill without spending any money as there are plenty of interesting cathedrals and street artists, plus the Gaudi buildings are just stuck between other normal houses in public thoroughfares. We located them all on our map and delighted in their weirdness. We would love to have gone inside but it was too expensive. We decided to head back to the car but wasted over an hour trying to find where we had parked. It was starting to get dark and we were walking around in circles. It was somewhere in the Eixample and beautiful as that area was architecturally (built in a strict grid-pattern with chamfered corners), it was like a trippy concrete giant maze and we had become three tiny Alices. After going down a few blind alleys we finally located the Renault 5, ran

over to it and hugged it.
We spent the evening in a town called Granollers which was buzzing due to some local elections and there was a stage set up in the main square with a band playing. In a bar, a group of local teenagers shouted "Hippy!" every time Flee went past as she was wearing John Lennon glasses, sandals and had long uncombed hair. What did she expect? I had my Thursday night call with Klaus who was interested to know where we were and he told us that we must go and visit Dali's house in Cadaqués en route to the French border. When we got back to our car we had what turned out to be an amusing flyer on our wind screen. It was a picture of the 'ERC' party candidate Eudald Balcells i Diaz and his election poster was him dressed in a dinner jacket and bow tie looking eerily like Freddie Mercury. We couldn't resist and wrote 'Freddie Mercury for President' along the top and a speech bubble coming out of his mouth singing 'Barcelona!'
Inside the car it was starting to get very hot now and we were sleeping on our sleeping bags rather than in them, and had taken to parking on the seafront so we could be awoken by majestic sunrises. We swam in the sea a lot and had showers on the beach, and cooked more food because we could sit outside in the evenings. We treated ourselves to grilled sardines on a few occasions because they were so cheap.
Next we headed up towards Girona, turning off at Figueres and driving down a windy, hair-raising road towards Roses and Cadaqués. Dali's house was situated in a little bay full of fishing boats; there was only one other house and a small hotel. It was a magical place. We walked down broken steps to find that it was all closed up for repairs so we had a peek over the garden wall and saw some sculptures. It was an old white-washed building with wooden doors that had been roughly painted, one of which was broken and a few slats were on the ground. We all took a piece of wood imagining that Salvador had probably painted his own doors, he was that eccentric. We drove back to Figueres in the hope of seeing the Dali expo in the local museum but that was also shut so we had a coffee in a bar which he'd frequented and then headed off in the direction of France. As we needed to get rid of our peseta coins, we stopped along the way and bought sweets and crisps before reaching the border and French customs:
"Have you got any hashish?" they said "How do you call it....shit? Yes shit. Have you got any shit?"
We said 'no' and then drove off. How very strange.
When you cross the frontier it's odd how you automatically know you are in France, it all just suddenly changes, no grey areas, no 'gently easing you in'. We motored along the coast and pulled in at Le Barcarès and towards the beach at Port Leucate. Immediately a hideous sight was there to behold – a large, white (but incredibly rusty) ship sunk into cement right on the beach. It was called 'Ly-

dia' and was now a night club/casino. It was an eyesore but also a curious folly, just sticking out like a sore thumb on an otherwise beautiful sandy beach. We parked up here for the night and made a pact that in the morning we would all take off our clothes and run into the sea, which we did. It was so warm that I didn't bother putting my clothes back on, nobody was around anyway and I wanted to get my bum brown. Later while I was sleeping (face down), Flee and Sark struck up a conversation with two blokes and a girl in a car nearby. The two blokes came back in the afternoon and came and sat with us, I was clothed by then. One was called Thierry (seemed to be a common name) and the other Pierre, who spoke good English. They were from Lyon and were here on holiday with a couple, Jean-Pierre & Frederique, and their baby Alexandre. They seemed like nice guys so we talked about Vieux Lyon which was where they happened to work in the catering trade and swapped stories about the bars and cafes we patronised when we 'lived' there in January. Pierre invited us to their house for a barbecue, he was the chef. They were very hospitable and friendly and we played Pétanque outside before having a Pastis aperitif and firing up the barby. Thierry called Flee 'Martian' because she didn't speak much and gradually we all got merry and had a good evening. I played a game of chess with Thierry, which lasted for over an hour, and won. To top it all they said we could go and get our sleeping bags and sleep on the floor, excellent!

In the morning, we ate croissants on the terrace for breakfast and Pierre invited us to stay for dinner again that evening as he was making moules. How lucky we were, it's just what we needed as we were starting to stagnate. However, it didn't take long for us to notice that Pierre had a bit of a problem. He was 33 and still lived with his parents, he rambled on, drew crap doodles which he thought was 'art', repeated himself endlessly and never listened to what anyone else said. He was a good cook though so we put up with his bossiness and enjoyed the moment, but he was starting to form an attachment to Sark and got her to help him with the washing up:

"Sarah, is there a man in your life?" droned Pierre.

"Nope," she clipped.

"We could be wonderful together you know," Pierre drooled.

Silence.

"Sarah, sleep with me tonight, just sleep next to me, in my bed, I promise that nothing, nothing at all will happen," begged Pierre.

"It's okay, thanks," snapped Sark

"Sarah, we are all dead already, I am, you are, you know that don't you," Pierre rambled on.

"Excuse me but I am very much alive, actually!" laughed Sark.

Pause.

"Sarah, I am closer to death than I am to life."

Pause.
“These plates are nice, aren’t they?” Sark said.
After dinner we played Yahtzee on the terrace and on Thierry’s last throw we gambled his lovely leather sandals as they fitted Sark perfectly and she needed them. We won and Sark now had footwear! As we were leaving the terrace, Thierry pulled me back inside and asked me to spend the night in his bed with him. I knew he had a thing for me, could see it in his eyes. Never beat a man at board games they always fall in love! He questioned why I was away from my husband and I tried to explain but he suddenly moved in for a kiss. I jumped back and he then grabbed me and held on to me saying “Pourquoi, pourquoi!” I have to admit that he was gorgeous and if I hadn’t been married, I would have taken him up on his offer. Pierre had adopted a very friendly ginger cat and had named him ‘Waddle’ after Chris Waddle, the football player; Waddle slept on the end of my sleeping bag that night. We had breakfast on the terrace and I read a bit of Stags and Hens by Willy Russell. We decided it was time to leave although they begged us to stay and insisted we left after lunch. Frederique took the baby to the beach and Jean-Pierre wanted to drive our car ‘for a laugh’ so we let him drive us to a fish market to buy oysters. After lunch we all said our goodbyes, Thierry grabbed my hand and held onto my wedding ring repeating “Pourquoi, pourquoi?” again. He didn’t give up! We were sorry to leave these people; they were all lovely, even mad Pierre was all right really. Sark started up the Renault 5 but the bugger wouldn’t go and they all had to push us down a hill. Eventually we got going and they all stood waving, getting smaller and smaller as we drove away.
We spent the night parked up near the sea under a full moon and had a discussion about where we thought a car’s genitals would be. Sark was talking about our ‘Guardian Angels’ who were figures, or symbols of those figures, that were helping us safely along our journey or giving us warnings. Sark was a bit spiritual like this and Flee and I took the piss out of her and wanted some concrete examples of these Guardian Angels. There were two types she explained; first there was ‘The Dead Soldier’. He could be an actual real soldier, a statue or a field of poppies and then there was Aslan, the Lion from Narnia. The Soldier had cropped up in Paris apparently, guiding us to park-up safely near barracks. Then he had taken the shape of a photo in the abandoned ruin in Ronda just before we got mugged. Aslan had now taken centre-stage because we kept seeing large ‘lion dogs’ who Sark swears always “turned and looked at her”. She was a total moon cookie. I said that one day I was going to write a film script of our journey and we could re-live the whole thing again but this time in luxury. We decided to call it ‘Tarmac and White Lines’ ‘cos that’s what we seem to see most of these days”. I couldn’t sleep so got out my sacred Walkman and stuck on a Bowie mix-tape that my old boyfriend Mark had put together for me years back entitled: ‘Various Excellent David Bowie Vinyl’.

Chapter Fourteen
Patrick and the Flat-Trick

Sark woke up singing Morning is Broken which although freaky was a nice change from one of her blackies. Alan had told us that a good place to work was Marseillan Plage, a small seaside town that had a lot of campsites. I only had thirty quid left so had to find something sharpish. Maybe we could find another boat opportunity like in Gibraltar. Maybe Black Danny would just pop his head out of a hatch somewhere and save the day. Alan had also told us to go and seek out "Willy and Julia in Pomérols", friends of his who ran a bar. We searched in vain but gave up so we walked around Marseillan, a nice simple place which had one of those tourist pottery shops that sold cups and saucers in the shape of penises and fannies and couples shagging. Why? They also sold them in Spain - vile! We tried to find work at some campsites but they said we needed permits and according to our book, the employers could easily obtain these from the local police. We weren't sure what the problem was and feeling dejected, we treated ourselves to our first French cake in months. We bought a beach tennis set with which to amuse ourselves and even gave Flee a driving lesson who was good considering our bad car. "Sark, you play tennis like a ballet dancer and dance like a tennis player," Flee remarked. An 'Aslan' dog kissed Sark's hand tonight; she said it must be a good sign.

Thursday night was Klaus night. He was very excited to report that he and Richard had lifted Meerschaum out of the water and he'd been given permission to park it on some barrels on the Europort building site free of charge. They'd already scraped off the barnacles and he could use all the power-tools from their container to do the work. The other juicy gossip was that Hawk has been confiscated by the police and Roy was living in his van! Apparently Roy had been 'looking after' a stolen boat all this time which he apparently wasn't aware of. Roy was always sailing close to the wind quite literally and he reminded me of my older brother Nick, in that he did tend to fabricate things and embroider the truth. He told us he was a DJ in England, amongst a myriad other professions that he was 'experienced' in. "Roy isn't really a DJ," Sark said, "He's just a knob who's got some records at home".

Klaus offered to send me some money if I needed it but I said no. We spent the rest of the evening in bar Lou Pescadou in Marseillan Plage concocting conspiracy theories about Roy and his dodgieness and got talking to yet another Thierry who ran the place, along with an English couple who had been holidaying there for years and who told me that 'Okay Pizza' next door were looking for staff. Later on, a short fat bloke came into the bar whom we'd seen earlier taking his cat for a walk. He was a 'mime-artist type' who kept making eyes at us theatrically, loved to drop his trousers and played with a packet of condoms. He'd converse with his cat by 'meowing' at it, so he got nicknamed Fatty Meow although his real name was actually Laurent. People kept buying us drinks and we all sat around talking. We also met a French chef called Patrick who worked at a nearby hotel. He lived alone in a flat which came with his job and he said we could all move in with him. In a drunken stupor we walked there nearly keeling over with our bags. The flat had terrible '70s decor but who was complaining. Our room had a set of bunk beds and another single bed that pulled down from the wall. Things were finally beginning to look up. In the morning and despite a terrible hangover, I had a shower, dressed as respectably as I could and went over to 'Okay Pizza' to ask for a job. It was a tiny little restaurant run by J-P and Marice, a husband and wife team. She did the cooking and he was the barman but also manned the pizza oven. To my delight, they gave me a job! I had to do a trial for a week to see how things went and they asked if I could translate the menu into English as they had a lot of English customers. So that night Patrick helped me do this back at the flat. It turned out that it was in fact quite a good traditional French restaurant but the 'Okay Pizza' name brought the tourists in and they did make proper pizzas in a traditional oven which were more than just 'okay'. Patrick taught us how to play 'gin rummy' and we had a few games while listening to 'Nostalgie', my new favourite French radio station which was much more up my street with old Serge Gainsbourg and Jacques Brel numbers played regularly. Patrick told us that he had two 'bastard children' one in England, the other in Switzerland- charming.

I loved my job, it was just J-P, Marice and I most days and sometimes a French girl called Clarice worked the lunch shift. I did a bit of everything, waitressing, washing-up and the dreaded mussel-scraping. I was getting to know the regulars: a gay couple who J-P always said "bonjour monsieur-dames" to, the factory girls who came for lunch and ate camembert, and my favourite, Alain, a large sagely man who propped up the bar, drank 51s and said that the English make "the best breakfasts in the world".

Flee, Sark and Patrick came in most nights, sometimes he treated them to dinner, other nights they just had a last drink with us when we finished for the evening. I was saving money fast and not spending any on food because I always ate at work. We had made friends in the square: Petit Tom who ran the bar opposite and wore Cuban heels and was still shorter than me. He was on our smarm-alarm hit list, Italian and sex-starved and always said Ooh La La La! (adding an extra 'La' every time); then there was the most handsome bloke in the world despite being oldish and grey-haired, Andre the Coquillage Man, who ran a shellfish stall in the daily market and had mesmerising blue eyes; then there was good old Thierry from Lou Pescadou and not forgetting our dear friend Fatty Meow. Sark and Flee decided to take Alan's advice and start a baguette business for beach-goers. They bought all the ingredients and made a good selection and wrapped them in foil to take to the beach to sell. We have been learning more about Patrick's life story and he showed us some of his papers which said veuf on them:
"Do you know what that means?" Asked Patrick.
"No," I said.
"I am a widower" He said after a knowing look.
"What happened?" I asked.
"My English wife died in a car crash on the M25, our son lives with her parents in London," He added coldly.
"What about the mother of your other child?" I asked.
"She's also dead, it's horrible," Patrick remarked then bowed his head.
Patrick didn't go into any more detail other than he said he was working at this hotel to earn money to send to his children, that he hated his boss but had to put up with him and they argued every day.
Unfortunately, the sandwich business failed miserably and Sark was in a blackie. They didn't sell anything and now the fridge was full of baguettes. Sark was running out of money but Flee still had enough as she had saved up a lot more of her Pizza Hut earnings than we had.
"What about that bag of money in the car Sark?" Flee enquired
"What bag of money in the car?" Sark seemed to be unaware.
"What do you mean 'what bag of money in the car?" Flee laughed in reply.
"That heavy, bulky, purple cotton bag of yours which we keep moaning about?" I chipped in.
"Oh that!" Sark laughed.
Flee and I had been complaining about this way back when we were in Toulouse and had told her to change all her centimes and francs before we left France and since then, this heavy bag of cash was a source of complaint which Sark then added to once we'd returned to France.

"Go and get it from the car now" Flee ordered
Sark obeyed and we emptied it out onto the table and counted it up. 30 quid in coins and she'd been carrying it around all this time! That night we played consequences at the flat. The game where we each write part of a story on a piece of paper, fold it over and then pass it on for the next person to write their bit on. The outcome is a sometimes amusing disjointed story:
Consequence No 1:
BOY'S NAME: Roy
GIRL'S NAME: Medusa
WHERE THEY MET: In that toilet with the stinking shit in Olvera
HE SAID TO HER: Wiggle It Just A Little Bit
SHE SAID TO HIM: It's up my fuckin arse
HE GAVE HER: His 'brushed across the pate' greasy hair
SHE GAVE HIM: An everlasting tooth impression on his 'little' Peter
AND THE CONSEQUENCE WAS: They all got fat and said meow
Consequence No 2:
BOY'S NAME: Fatty Meow
GIRL'S NAME: Sarah wet look Gee string
WHERE THEY MET: Lobo
HE SAID TO HER: Hey foxy lady where's the beach?
SHE SAID TO HIM: Yes, but shave my pubes off first
HE GAVE HER: A load of bullshit about how manly he was
SHE GAVE HIM: A kiss on his fat bum
AND THE CONSEQUENCE WAS: The green, green grass was in the stomach of the yellow cow who got fucked by a Nord
Consequence No 3:
BOY'S NAME: Fatty Meow
GIRL'S NAME: Claire Perry
WHERE THEY MET: In Petit Tom's stacked heels
HE SAID TO HER: Tu faire l'amour dans le lit avec moi?
SHE SAID TO HIM: Yes darling
HE GAVE HER: Two flans and a mille feuille
SHE GAVE HIM: An open oyster to lick then swallow
AND THE CONSEQUENCE WAS: We all live in a yellow submarine
Things had changed and I was mostly at work now while the girls were at home or on the beach topping up their tans trying to avoid Patrick because although he was doing us a favour, he sort of played on the fact and expected to spend all his spare time with us. I was busy but I was missing Klaus terribly and the Thursday phone calls were getting emotional. He wanted me to come back and I wanted to go back but I didn't want to leave Flee and Sark on their own. I talked to

them about it and they said that I must go back if I was feeling that way and they would be fine by themselves and anyway, Paul had written to say he'd be coming down to visit us on 24th June so they had that to look forward to. Patrick helped me plan my return trip and went and bought me a flight ticket on his credit card and said that I could pay him back once he had picked it up.
I did love living in Marseillan-Plage, the weather was glorious and I would get up for work and walk around the corner to the restaurant. Petit Tom would always be there standing in his doorway singing that Paul Young song 'Senza una donna'. Work was starting to become a bit of a pain because J-P had a drink problem and a foul temper especially when we weren't busy. I was starting to feel like Manuel from Fawlty Towers because he and Marice were always arguing and he would take it out on me and lose his patience with my limited French. There were good times though when the place was full and Alain was at the bar. One morning Clarice was polishing the glasses, J-P was in a good mood making some pizza dough with Marice and 'Nostalgie' was on the radio. A Serge Gainsbourg song came on and J-P jumped to the radio and turned it up full volume. Everyone carried on with their chores in time with the music and sang along to every word; once it was over they turned the radio back down and carried on as normal.
"What was that song?" I asked
"Le Poinçonneur des Lilas" Alain explained. "It's a song about the ticket-puncher at Lilas underground station in Paris who spends his days bored stiff wishing he was somewhere else and how all he does is punch 'little holes' in tickets and how one day he wants to put a 'little hole' in his head and then be put in a 'big hole' in the ground." "Little holes, little holes" were the lyrics of the chorus and Alain sang the catchy tune back to me:
J´fais des trous, des p´tits trous, encor des p´tits trous
Des p´tits trous, des p´tits trous, toujours des p´tits trous

"You like Gainsbourg Rebecca?" asked Alain
"I love him!"
"I cannot believe that an English girl likes Gainsbourg, this is incredible!" Alain was delighted.
Later that afternoon, Alain came back and gave me two Serge Gainsbourg cassettes, one of which included the song that he'd sung along to with such animation earlier that day. What a lovely gesture. I gave Flee another driving lesson that day.
That evening Patrick told us that he'd had an argument with his boss and finally quit his job at the hotel and had already found another job in a rival hotel but that he had paid for the flat until the end of the month so we could still live the-

re. That was kind of him. I told J-P and Marice that I would be leaving soon so that they could find a replacement for me. I hadn't set a date yet because Patrick hadn't given me the tickets but I guessed I'd still be there for a few more weeks. A couple of days later I returned home one afternoon to find Sark and Flee being booted out of the flat standing downstairs by the car and speaking in monotone unison:
Me: Hello.
Sark & Flee: Hello.
Me: What's happening?
Sark & Flee: We are being chucked out.
Me: Who by?
Sark & Flee: Some bloke, he's upstairs.
Me: Where is he?
Sark & Flee: Upstairs.
It was the grumpy manager of the hotel and he'd made them chuck everything in the car shouting "Vite maintenenant!" I had some wet clothes soaking in a bucket which I had to quickly wring out and the manager watched over us as we cleared the flat muttering to us in angry French. We went straight to Petit Tom's and told everyone about it and Alain drove us round to the hotel and spoke to the manager who told him that Patrick hadn't quit - he had been sacked because he was useless and the flat was for his new chef and Patrick had not 'paid for it till the end of the month'. Then Alain drove to the restaurant in Agde where Patrick was now working. Patrick lost his temper, said the manager was lying and that he'd come to Thierry's tonight and 'explain everything' but he never showed up and we never saw him again.
We all sat in Petit Tom's talking about Patrick, and Alain concluded that he was a 'bullshitter' and all those stories he told us were probably lies and that he hadn't bought me flight tickets. Luckily I hadn't given him any money for them. We now had to go back and sleep in the car which was not ideal because I was working and needed to be clean and tidy. We decided to go and stay on the campsite but as it was gone midnight, Petit Tom stepped in and let us stay in his empty flat although we could only have it for one night as he had let it out to some people who were arriving the following day. The next morning at work, Alain told me he had been to the campsite and paid for us to stay at Mini Camping La Parisienne until the end of the month. He also gave me a carton of 200 cigarettes - "anything for an English girl who loves Gainsbourg!" he said.

Chapter Fifteen
Old Friends

The one good thing to come out of this was that we found a 2-man tent in Patrick's flat which we took with us when we were being kicked out, and we made a replacement pole for our own tent out of a bit of wood. Sark and I slept in one and Flee the other one. Paul was arriving soon so we thought that arrangement would be more sensible although Flee wasn't sure how he'd feel about it. The campsite was small but full of friendly folk; a German couple with a cherub child and some elderly Irish people in a caravan. The wife looked like Mrs Mangle off Neighbours and stayed inside all the time and he was an annoying chatterbox. We all washed our cacks in the sinks and then hang them out to dry on the washing lines and the Irish perve remarked to Flee "what pretty underwear you all have."
Sark finally found work as a general helper at Hippocamp and started immediately. I had a day off work so Flee and I thought we would go to the infamous nudey beach at Camp d'Agde and as soon as we parked up we saw a naked man walking around the car park. It wasn't so much a nudist beach but a nudist complex, they were everywhere, in telephone boxes, riding bicycles and even shopping in the mini-market. We kept our kit on until we reached the beach which was packed with nudies - all bollocks, arseholes, clits and tits and we quickly shoved on our sunglasses so we could take in the panorama without offending anyone. It was liberating swimming in the sea naked and we struck up a conversation with a young couple from London who probably thought we were lezzies. Later, a funny looking bloke wearing glasses and carrying a brief case and a plastic carrier bag came and sat behind us:
"Hello, are you English?" The weirdo asked.
"Yes," we replied nervously.
"Would you mind if I take a photo of you?" He smiled sweetly, sickly.
"Alright," we let out slowly.

(We were both lying down so didn't care)
"Now can you both go into the sea so I can take a photo of you coming out wet?" The sickly smile again.
"Fuck right off!" We shouted, and he scuttled off down the beach.
That evening two letters had arrived, a lovely long emotional one from Klaus who couldn't wait for me to get home and another one from Yumi who told me that Bruno and Irwin had left Brighton and moved to France and gave me a contact address. Bruno was living in Agde! Tonight was the last shift I would work at Okay Pizza as I needed time to organise things and I wanted to enjoy my last few days with the girls before leaving them for who knows how long.
The next morning Flee and I dropped Sark off at Hippocamp and drove to Agde. We went to the travel agents where I bought my flight ticket from Barcelona to Malaga, for Wednesday 26th June, and also organised a train ticket from Béziers to Barcelona. With a map from the travel agent, we located Bruno's street which led us onto a tiny square surrounded by beautiful old buildings. I stopped an old woman and showed her the address and she called up to an open window. Seconds later Bruno popped his head out: "Rebecca, is that really you?" Flee and I raced upstairs and it was hugs all round. We had coffee with them and Bruno kept laughing and calling me 'Madame Rebecca' and they invited us round for dinner the next evening. Bruno's dinners were always memorable.
Sark was in the tent reading when we got back and she told us that she'd been sexually harassed by our Irish pensioner neighbour who'd come over to her tent and asked if she had any 'sexual fantasies' he could carry out for her: "You know dear, something your boyfriend wouldn't do to you". What a complete and utter slime!
We sat around sunbathing on the grass in front of our tents listening to 'Nostalgie' and heard something familiar on the radio. "Isn't this that Jimmy Somerville song?" I asked, "you know, the wipe your bum with a tissue song?" It was indeed the original version of 'Comment te dire adieu' and it wasn't a 'Jimmy Somerville song' after all. It was sung by a French woman called Françoise Hardy.
I called Charlie's that night even though it wasn't Thursday, perchance Klaus would be in there and so he was! I gave him my flight details and he said he would borrow Edgar's car and collect me. We were so excited to finally be seeing each other again; I had spent more time away from him than I'd ever spent with him and almost forgotten what he looked like.
Sark was working late the next day so she couldn't go to Bruno's which was a shame for her but she was being kept entertained by Dishy Doug, the Scotsman, who worked at Hippocamp. We arrived at Bruno & Irwin's to find them sun-tanned and relaxed in their fabulous flat. Bruno was much happier to be back in France because now he could grow "house trees". They gave us Whiskey & Coke in large tumblers and then served us up a delicious regional meal and he told Flee that she

must come back anytime she wanted and to bring Sark along, too. We drank long into the night, then said our farewells, Bruno promising to come to Gibraltar en route to a planned tour of Morocco.

Paul was arriving that day so Flee and I dropped Sark at work and then headed towards Béziers railway station to pick him up. We got there early and had a wander around; it was another beautiful French town with lovely shops and buildings. We swooned over gorgeous pairs of shoes and treated ourselves in the patisserie. I was really going to miss France and all the wonderful food. It was very hot these days so we lounged in a park and discussed Paul and what his visit might or might not bring, it was all rather ambiguous. At the station his train pulled in and there he was. He just fell into Flee's arms and started to cry and then came over and gave me a tearful hug; we'd all been friends since school and had spent many a memorable moment together. We drove back to Marseillan Plage to pick up Sark from work and found her sitting in a bar outside with none other than Alan! He'd finally left Gibraltar and was on his way to Denmark with his mate Peter and thought he would stop off and see if he could find us. The six of us had a drink and a catch-up and laughed about the failed baguette business and then Alan and Peter needed to get on the road so left. Alan was a proper diamond.

Sark and I had decided to leave Flee and Paul on their own for a bit so we went out for a drink. Sark mentioned that she didn't think she'd be working much longer at Hippocamp because they had enough staff already and there wasn't a lot for her to do. We got back to the campsite and Flee and Paul were already in her tent - he obviously didn't object to the sleeping arrangements after all.

Mardi 25 Juin. It was my last day in France and the last day with my friends. Sark told us of her dream where Paul had something wrong with his balls and she had to squeeze them open like oysters to try and rectify them. Sark had to work which was a shame so Flee, Paul and I all bundled into the Renault 5 and drove into Agde to buy food and wine for a celebratory last meal, then spent the rest of the day on the beach. I finally found out who'd sent that telegram to me on my wedding day - it was Matthew, Paul's elder brother. There was always talk about him liking me and I liked him too, a lot actually, but it never quite happened and then I left England anyway. Matt was travelling around America and according to Paul was apparently 'gutted' that I'd got married. Oh well, 'the one that got away' is what Matthew Churchill would remain to me.

Later that day, Sark got back with the bad news that her job had indeed finished so she was upset until we showed her the food we had bought for tonight. We all tucked in and got pissed together and went down to the beach and looked up at the stars. We had a night-cap at Petit Tom's and introduced Paul to Fatty Meow who danced around in front of him hand-on-heart doing Arnold Schwarzenegger impressions and poses.

Chapter Sixteen
Rod Stewart

I packed up all my stuff into my trusty rucksack and put it in the boot before going to Place du Marche one final time to say goodbye to all our friends: Thierry the bar owner; Petit Tom and his stacked heels (Oooh La La La!); Andre the Coquillage Man; J-P & Marice; Clarice; the factory girls and their camembert; the wonderful and generous Alain and last but not least Fatty Meow. They all came out to wave me goodbye and wished me well, demanding that I return with Klaus for a holiday soon. Sark drove us to Béziers and swore blind that there was a 'knock-knock-knock' on the side of the car just as we drove past a monument of a soldier. "The Dead Soldier is back! Though we hadn't see Aslan for a while" Sark squealed with delight. We explained the meaning of this madness to Paul and made our way to the station and waited on the platform in silence. Nobody knew what to say really. The train pulled in and Paul had to help me with my bag as it was so heavy and I couldn't lift it onto my back. Before I knew it, the automatic doors started closing and I gave them all a quick kiss and the train slowly pulled away and I watched as their three waving figures faded into the distance. I slumped down into my seat and just stared out of the window in a daze which lasted for hours. I had spent most of my life having a relationship with Sark and Flee and although in these past years we lived in different cities, we kept in touch by letter or telephone and would spend many weekends plus all the important holidays together. They meant the world to me and had been a constant these last few months and I suddenly felt horribly alone. How long would it be until I saw them again? I wondered how far they would get in the car. The Renault 5 was behaving itself perfectly ever since Klaus had fixed it but I wasn't sure how it was going to fare in extreme temperatures. But I also missed Gibraltar and was eager to get back there and start a new life. I knew then that I would never return to live in England - I had known that ever since I was a small child but I had never known exactly where I would end up or what I would do. I would have to find a job, didn't really want to go back and work at Pizza Hut. This was my proper life now and I had to start thinking sensibly. What was married life really going to be like? Was Richard still living on the boat with Klaus? We couldn't all live there together, not now, the boat was tiny and Klaus and I needed privacy and space. I was so anxious to see Klaus again but at the same time so nervous, it had all happened so quickly and it was all so intense. I had been living such a free life with Sark and Flee, there were no pressures, we had lived an idyll in the South of France in beautiful summer weather. We'd had some scrapes and adventures but everything was light and fun and laid-back. Nothing had sunk in; I just had that image of them standing on the platform at Béziers station, so rudely taken away from me with the abrupt closing of those awful, mechanical train doors. No time to cry.

Eventually I arrived at Barcelona Sants and had to hoist up my heavy bag and find a connecting train for the airport. There wasn't a lot of time to locate the right platform and buy a ticket, the train from Béziers had arrived at 10.15 and I had to be at the airport at 10.55. I managed to get the tickets but had to find the right train and this involved running up and down some steps and at one point I fell over with the bag and two men had to help me up. I was in tears by then but had to keep going. Finally I got on the train but it didn't leave until 10.30 and I wasn't sure how long the journey took or where to go when I got to the airport. I leapt off when it pulled in and grabbed a trolley to get respite from the weight of the bag and ran to check-in and onto to Gate 8 and boarded the plane just in time. What a relief, I was finally on my way home! I got out 'To The Lighthouse' and read for the whole journey. What was it going to be like seeing Klaus after all this time? I had indeed been away longer than I had actually known him. I felt terribly nervous - not least for having to spend the night with him. It almost felt like an arranged marriage. There I was, going back to a strange land and would be spending the rest of my life with a man I hardly knew. Was Klaus feeling the same way?

I landed at Malaga on time and waited for my rucksack at the baggage carousel and walked into the arrivals hall scanning for Klaus but I couldn't see him. Where was he? typical Klaus always late. I could not believe that he was not there to greet me; I had expected a romantic reunion at arrivals. The hall started to clear and I was loathe to put that heavy bag on my back again so went to get a trolley and discovered I did not have a 100 peseta coin. I was exhausted and emotional. Where was Klaus? Was there another terminal at Malaga airport, had he gone to the wrong one by mistake? No, I was sure there was only one arrivals hall at this airport and Klaus was very familiar with Malaga, he'd been here loads of times. I dragged my bag into the toilet cubicle as I was dying to go and when I came out of the loos, there was still no sign of Klaus. I didn't want to leave that area just in

case he appeared. A message hollered over the tannoy but it was just announcing another landing. It was past 1am and I was starting to get worried. Why would Klaus be so late? Dejected I flung my rucksack onto the floor and used it as a cushion to sit on. I was disorientated and feeling very strange on my own without Flee and Sark. Then in the distance I noticed a vaguely familiar and lanky figure running towards me and it was him! He was all tanned and his hair had grown a lot and was bleached by the sun. The tash had gone (always hated that thing) and he actually looked like Rod bloody Stewart. I quickly shook that image out of my head and ran over to him for a lovely long kiss. He'd been driving around for ages, trying to find somewhere to park because he didn't have the right change for the machine and didn't want to risk getting clamped. I doubted this was the real reason for this lateness but now we were reunited, I didn't want to question him and spoil the moment. Excited, he told me that we weren't going to sleep on the boat that night as Edgar had arranged for us to stay at Europa Point We drove back talking all the way, passing many of the places the girls and I had visited earlier that year. This time there was no confusion trying to find the turning for Gibraltar and how wonderful it was to see the Rock in all its majesty as we got closer to home. I had missed that funny little place. We stopped off at Ramsons to get a takeaway, headed for the point and Sunflower House and finally made it to bed at some unearthly hour. The next morning Klaus handed me a small red box and inside was a gold ring shaped as a reef knot, "It's to symbolise the knot of our friendship," he said, "I am never going to let you go away again, you are tied to me forever," and so he put it on my finger next to my wedding ring.
Later on, Roy turned up to say hello. It was his last day at work tomorrow and he was going back to England so I filled him in with our news and we said our goodbyes. Edgar came home, no kisses or hugs from him - just "let's go out to dinner in Bianca's for Steak-Chips-Pepper-Sauce," which we did.
Flee and Sark had until the end of June in the campsite, courtesy of Alain, and for two days after I left, Sark had to 'play gooseberry' with Flee and Paul which wasn't pleasant because they were either shagging in the tent or spitting-out bitter comments to one another. Paul lent them thirty quid though which was a blessing. They had breakfast at Bruno's and he helped them with information about fruit picking jobs and made some calls to farms further along the coast who said they had work to offer. So they packed up all the stuff from the campsite, went and said goodbye to the Place du Marche gang and headed off to Sète. They arrived at the place that Bruno had telephoned but were greeted with blank expressions and told there was "no work". They got back into the car and decided just to head straight for Marseille. Money was really, really low and they had started to eat only bread with raw onions and a bit of vinegar sprinkled on top which was all that was left in the food basket. They didn't even have enough

money to buy any laughing cow cheese.
Along the road to Marseille they approached Arles and were suddenly surrounded by apricot trees for miles so pulled into the town and went in search of work. Again nothing doing so they started out for Marseille the next morning but the car didn't start. It died on them, they tried everything but it just would not start and they'd spent precious money on petrol the day before.
They eventually caved in and made a reverse-charge call to their parents and asked for money to be sent over so they could go back to England. The travel insurance had nearly run out anyway and it was time to simply 'go home'. Pam organised a wire-transfer to Crédit Agricole in Arles but it could take at least a week, they only had enough money to buy two more baguettes and the gas had run out so no tea or coffee either. They were living off tap water, bread and vinegar by this point and had taken to nicking coins out of fountains so they could buy fags and have a coffee in a bar to alleviate the boredom. Eventually it even got to the point where they were scanning the floor for suitably long discarded fag butts to smoke. Sark said they walked around the whole of Arles "about twenty-five times" and that it was boiling, sleeping in the car, and the 'library' had been exhausted and she'd taken to reading Eastern Europe on a Shoestring, as a last resort. They'd had the wherewithal earlier on to buy some dice and pieced together a home-made backgammon board drawn on paper, using stones as playing pieces, and would sit under the trees in the square, playing game upon game, with an audience of young scallywags. Sark then had a stroke of luck and found a 100 Franc note on the ground so that kept them going until the money finally arrived; no doubt Aslan was in the vicinity. They promptly bought two pieces of flan, fags and train tickets in that order.
Monday 10th June 1991. After a night spent living-it-up in a restaurant and then feeling sick afterwards, Sark and Flee packed up their rucksacks and got on the train to Gare du Nord, a journey which was not uneventful; Sark got her feet fondled by a bloke on the train, Flee had her whole body fondled at night in the dark having to shove the perpetrator away shouting "FUCK OFF", and in the morning a man angrily rapped on the toilet door while Flee was pissing shouting "Samantha, Samantha!" They changed in Paris for a train to Calais then got on a cross-channel ferry but when they saw the White Cliffs of Dover their hearts sank. Were they really back in England after such an adventure? Everything looked strange and the number plates seemed massive. When they got to Emsworth it felt like they had been away for either ten years or maybe just ten minutes...
Our Renault 5 was parked up under a tree in a picturesque square in Arles, the old stomping-ground of Van Gogh, a "very fitting and lovely spot" Flee said. The 'library' still lay along the back shelf with the gas burner and camping gear in

the boot. They had left the keys in the ignition so she was there for anyone who fancied her; she was home at last too.

The End